DEX'S WAY

Karina Fabian

LASER COW PRESS

Laser Cow Press

Merritt Island, FL

Laser Cow Press
Merritt Island, FL
https://fabianspace.com

Book Layout © 2017 BookDesignTemplates.com
Cover art by Dawn Grimes

Dex's Way/Karina Fabian. -- 1st ed.
Print ISBN: 978-1-7334471-4-0

For those who are struggling to understand the future holds for them and for our world. Where there is life, there is hope. Where there is hope, there is a better future.

Author Note:

*If you've not read **The Old Man and the Void**, may I suggest you do so first? You'll enjoy **Dex's Way** that much more!*
- Karina

Contents

Prologue

The ship shook, threatening to knock Dex to the ground as he struggled to get on the VR gloves and headset that connected him to the *Santiago*'s control systems. There was no way Santiago was going to get them out of this battle alone, much less escape the event horizon of the black hole. He needed Dex Hollister as much as Dex needed him.

And we both needed that damn Civ B ship that got us into this mess in the first place. Don't lose it, he willed the *Santiago* as he adjusted the straps to the headgear. *Don't let it go.*

The immediate view of his blasted-apart bridge disappeared, replaced by a rudimentary navigational display of the nearby space and a control panel for the ship's systems. A simple diagram showed his ship, the *Santiago*, connected by thin lines to the larger alien warship from the civilization they called Civ B. Behind them, a small swarm of drone ships from Civ A converged upon them. He called for a status update from the AI. Above and ahead of them was a thin line that represented the boundary they had to cross to escape the black hole.

"Capture beams are holding. We're still tied to the Civ B ship," Santiago reported. "The Civ A drones are continuing their attack. We are undergoing heavy damage. The Civ B ship is heading toward the event horizon, taking us with it, but I think it has lost navigation control."

As the ship spoke, Dex activated his controls. The world around him grew, changed color, and came alive with flashes of light and streaking phantoms of dark, and he was with Santiago, seeing through his sensors, feeling the impact of radiation and energy on his hull. The enemy ships had moved out of the targeting area of Santiago's laser, but the AI was laying a covering pattern that would keep the drones themselves away from where they could target the vulnerable backup engineering section. On one side of the screen, he saw the twisting energies where the millennia of battle between the ships of the long-dead aliens who called themselves "the People" had disrupted spacetime on both sides of the black hole.

Dex smiled ferally. They were going to make it back to their universe and with the captured Civ B ship or die trying. "Then we're telling it where to go. All we need are its shields and its engines to carry us through the event horizon, anyway. See the swarls?" he asked Santiago as he traced a route through the anomalies that swirled and twisted like clockwork gears made of spacetime. "We're going to ride the swarls out of here."

A pause. Again, the ship jerked and shuddered as Santiago jinked away from a laser shot Dex hadn't seen, then suffered the brunt of the explosion it caused on their prey. He put weight on his broken leg as he caught his balance and fought his own battle against a red miasma of pain.

"Hull breach, small airlock and adjoining storage," the secondary computer reported. "Blocking off areas."

"Drone targeted—direct hit," Santiago chimed in. Despite everything, Dex imagined he heard a smug tone in the AI's voice.

"Perfect the course!" he snapped at the AI. Their best hope for winning—for survival—was to escape to their own universe. Decades of experience navigating the accretion disk of a black hole had honed his navigational skill, but it took the computational power of an AI to manage the details. Without Santiago's input, he was dead.

The AI replied mildly. "I can multitask. But with imprecise sensors and all our damage–"

"Do it!"

"Firing torpedo. Engaging thrusters. Brace yourself."

He grabbed the arms of the cargo bot that was helping him stay upright as the *Santiago* applied all its power toward turning the captured ship on which they depended. He felt his ship's efforts in the vibrations of the deck; then, a sudden weight pressed him against flooring and robot as they were caught in the swarl.

"You did it! Pursuers?"

"Four."

"Get the next torpedo ready. I want it out and starboard on my signal." His hands flew before him, tracing the *Santiago's* projected path, then breaking away from it to show his planned route for the weapon.

"Right into the pod of drones," he muttered, "and no way for them to avoid it without getting thrown back the way we came. Ready? At your best time, my friend."

"Ready. Approaching new current..."

Dex's breathing sounded loud to his ears. The ship had stilled. The drones were slowing—did they suspect? But they continued in their pursuit, just as he'd anticipated.

"Launching torpedo. Hard to port. They're firing on us!"

This time the shock of motion threw Dex to the ground. The computer reported another hull breach.

Santiago said. "Sheilds failing. Dex, suit up!"

The repair bot raced to him, his suit gloves in its grasp. He snatched them, yanked them on, and reached for his helmet.

"Santiago! Talk to me! Shields?" He threw on the helmet and pressed the seals shut.

"Event horizon in nine...eight..."

Gravitational forces took hold of every cell in his body and pulled, and the last of Santiago's countdown was drowned out by his screams.

Everything around him, everything within him, tore, and he felt himself set afire then extinguished in the vacuum of space.

Dex woke up with his head in Scarlet's lap.

"Am I in heaven?" he murmured.

She laughed and stroked his hair. "You don't have a more original come-on than that?"

"I'm serious." It was the only explanation to have felt such pain and then awakened to the smiles of his long-dead wife. But he couldn't put much energy into his protest. He wanted to look around—he tried to look around—but everything except Scarlet was bathed in a cool, white glow. He could almost see his body, but his eyes refused to focus beyond a general blur. Was it because he was still old, injured, and partly blind, or did his heavenly body need time to adjust to its surroundings? Scarlet, too, was little more than a hazy shadow backlit by brilliant light.

She chuckled. "Not heaven, not in the literal sense, though you gave us a scare. But I am real, and so are you. Now, rest. I'll stay a while longer."

Rest. Hadn't he said when this was over, he wanted to sleep for a week? Rest sounded so good.

He allowed floating numbness to take over him and followed Scarlet's soothing caresses into a comfortable nothing.

* * *

Dex awoke on the Bloody Road, trapped in the sticky mud, barely able to move. Scarlet was gone, and the wonderful numbness he'd felt in her arms was gone. Pain slashed through his body, making him shake and gasp.

He moaned. "Scarlet!"

"Shhh." Again, cool hands caressed his brow, but they offered little relief. He thrashed against his captivity. The world was swathed in red and black, and fear joined course with the pain.

"Elomij!" he called to the alien goddess who had always shown herself in these visions. "Where are you? Help me," he shouted. He felt a sob but refused, even then, to let it out. He would not give her consort Hudon the satisfaction of seeing human frailty.

Again, a feminine voice shushed him, but he couldn't identify it. He heard other voices, murmurings of the dead. Were they angels urging him to heaven or demons drawing him to hell? The mindless victims of Hudon's game, wandering aimlessly without the ability to continue their battles? No. Those were myths, stories he'd listened to while trying to repair Santiago. Was he hallucinating again?

That meant he was alive, but if he was alive, why couldn't he move?

The words combined with his agony, confusing him. He fought to latch onto something he could focus on. Something real.

A shape, dark and backlit. Then reality shifted, and he saw Hudon—no longer resplendent in glory but tainted from his courtship with Corsha, the goddess of death. The sight of the alien god sparked anger in Dex, and he zeroed in on it like the *Santiago's* targeting laser and let the anger give him strength.

"Hudon! Damn you. I've had enough of your games! I beat your drones. I showed my worth. I'm not one of your pawns. Let me go!"

Hudon spoke, cool and emotionless. "Enough. Put him down."

"No! Let me go!"

He jerked his head up and out of the quagmire. Hands caught his face, covered his nose and mouth, pressed him back. He bucked and fought, desperation giving him strength and superseding the pain, but phantom hands rose from the Bloody Road and held him fast. He felt himself sinking into the mud.

Even though he knew it was futile, he screamed and struggled until the road had claimed him and again, he was swept into nothingness.

Chapter One

Dex opened his eyes to glaring white. For a moment, he thought Hudon had killed him. Then, shadow and line brought definition, and he saw the joins of ceiling to walls. Colors returned, the glare settling into the light, steely gray of gabrium alloy. He couldn't move his head, but in his peripheral vision, he saw tubes and monitors with flashing lights and symbols too blurry to make out.

He was lying in a bed in a hospital room.

"We made it," he whispered, with a small, bemused laugh.

"Verification," a mellow voice said, and he felt a hand touch him reassuringly. "Verification. Correction: singular, projective."

Yes, but only you, his mind translated. With difficulty, he moved his eyes toward the speaker. Pale skin covered cheekbones too angular and pronounced to be human. A full lower lip jutted from below a too-thin upper one. Eyes large and dark with slit pupils. A cascade of thick lustrous hair, a mellow shade of brown. A slight body with curves that suggested femininity. Two arms. The hand on his shoulder had only three fingers and an opposable thumb, longer than the others.

"What are you?" His voice cracked, and he coughed.

"Shhh." Cool hands caressed his brow, and a straw was placed against his lips. Reflexively, he pulled it into his mouth and sipped. The warm liquid bathed his mouth and soothed his throat, and he swallowed twice more before pulling away.

"Time pinpoint approximate reality misplacement projective in singularity?"

He started to say he didn't understand, then it came to him: *When did you disappear into the black hole?* He racked his brains for a date that seemed like a lifetime ago now and gave her the latest one he could remember.

The alien reared back with a gasp. She excused herself and fled the room.

He didn't care. Even that small conversation had drained him. If he was stranded among a bunch of aliens, there wasn't much he could do about it. Not without more sleep. At least the pain had gone.

* * *

The next few days continued much the same. He awoke, spoke a few words, returned to sleep. First, he did so without choice; then, to escape the confusion of the alien reality he found himself in; and sometimes, simply for the sheer luxury of being able to sleep. He wondered if he was being drugged. It would explain the lack of pain and how he could be comfortable remaining so still. He never dreamed as far as he could remember; he never pondered his survival; any time he thought to ask about the *Santiago* or the ship they'd captured, the thoughts fled into drowsiness. He couldn't even bring himself to care about his apparent paralysis, even though he still couldn't move other than to twist his neck. His body lay covered in a tightly fitted sheet, as if he were an infant in swaddling. Like an infant, he slept.

Then came the day he awoke to find a human at his bedside.

The man waited, patient and still but grinning like he wanted to jump up and shout with delight. Dex recognized the expression, the pent-up excitement. He'd felt the same way the first time he'd "met" Santiago. He looked about the same age Dex had been then, too: old enough to have seen some tragedy, but young enough for adventure. The way the man's blue eyes sparkled, Dex suspected he was this stranger's next adventure.

"Can you understand me?" the visitor asked.

Those weren't the words, exactly, but the small snatches of "conversation" in his lucid periods had accustomed him to automatically translating, and indeed, it was closer to Standard than anything he'd heard since the accident.

Dex nodded.

"Still, I am amazed! Lost since before the Unification, and yet you speak Fusion. I see now how the Elomijans could believe you to be the Huntradex."

"What?" Even though he understood the words, Dex had no idea what this man was talking about. The man continued to chatter excitedly about Dex being the "oldest" survivor of time dilation and what an enigma he was, but the more he talked, the less Dex understood. Suddenly, he wanted to sleep again, but sleep would not come.

So, he had been drugged. Had he been hallucinating, too? Were the aliens real? What about seeing Elomij on the Bloody Road. No, that had could not have been real. Where was he—and what was Unification?

He must have spoken aloud, for the man stopped his babbling to answer. "Oh, my apologies! This must be confusing to you. Fault reflexive, fault reflexive! Let me begin again. I am Georj Brenna. You are in the hospital complex at Keldar Station."

"Keldar? It's still here? I mean, how long...?"

"Please, keep yourself calm. It has been about 635 years, objective, as you would have kept time in your era."

"Six centuries. Huh. How about that?"

"You...do not seem surprised?"

Dex couldn't tell if this George Brenna was pleased or disappointed. They must still have people who patrolled or even hunted relics in the accretion disk of the black hole, so the effects of time dilation would be well known. People could leave for a mission and come back in what they would think were only weeks, but months and even years would have passed for the universe outside the influence of the black hole. Hence, the classification of "subjective" and "objective" time. But six centuries was probably a stretch of the imagination. Dex would not have thought it possible, but of course, he hadn't thought it possible to cross the event horizon of a black hole, and he'd done it not once, but twice.

"Not as surprised as I am to find Keldar still here." It was a comforting thought. Keldar had orbited the black hole, serving the scientists that studied it and the relic hunters who pulled wreckage from its grasp. It provided more than an infrastructure for science and exploration. For those that traveled into the accretion disk and experienced the disorientation of time dilation, it was a point of stability. Every run meant losing decades of objective time. Children grew old, lovers moved on, technology and culture advanced—all in what the traveler thought was only a short there-and-back. But no matter what, they knew they could depend on Keldar waiting for them when they returned.

Apparently, even after 600 years.

Brenna smiled. "Not the same complex, of course. Keldar has been rebuilt three times since you last saw it, at least if the date of your origin is as you told the nurses. Oh, how different it must have been then. There is a museum in my home world. My father took me there as a child. I was so fascinated by the displays of the ancient technology. I would set my hands into the sleeves of a VR unit..."

Dex moaned. He was remembering now: any time he'd managed the energy to ask a question, the person would either flee or launch into a long personal story until sleep again had taken Dex.

"Are you in pain?"

"Only from your incessant chatter. Tell me about Keldar."

Instead, the man tilted his head so that one ear rested on his shoulder, and brushed his blond hair aside, revealing his neck. "Fault reflexive, fault reflexive. Projective implorement of forgiveness."

"Yes, yes! Apology accepted. Just, tell me about Keldar. Short summary."

"Relief projective. Your grasp of Fusion is so adept, and in my excitement, I had forgotten how little you understand our culture. So much has changed."

"Start with Keldar."

"Yes, yes. This complex—" He waved his arms to indicate the station. "—is 125 years old, by your time's reckoning. It houses over 500,000 of the People—Elomijan and Human."

"The People?" Dex squawked. In his surprise, he tried to sit up, and found, for a wonder, that he could lift his shoulders until the swaddling held him down. Monitors picked up his distress and sounded alarms.

Brenna looked even more panicked than he felt. The young man leaned forward and pressed him back against the pillows. "Please, excite yourself not. Otherwise, they will again sedate you."

"I've slept enough!" he hollered for whatever monitors might be picking up his voice. He was sure, as a 600-year-old relic, he was being monitored, and not just for his health.

"Agreement emphatic! For weeks, our conversations have been little more than the exchange of a phrase or two. It is a joy and a relief to see you so lucid. But you must remain calm."

So, they had spoken before? He didn't remember it but filed the information away. Right now, another concern gnawed at him.

"Tell me about the People. Are we at war?" His heart hammered at the thought, and his mind filled with the vision of a long road of blood-soaked dirt.

Brenna laughed. "Oh, no! These are not the People whose relics you long hunted. These are the offshoot, devoted to Elomij and embracing change without the destructive competition that destroyed their brothers.

Approximately forty years after your disappearance, the first treaties between Humans and Elomijans were signed. The Unification. We are now a single People. Over the centuries, the Elomijans had a pacifying effect on much of the human race, as well."

"Then why am I imprisoned? Drugged into submission?" He jerked again at his bonds. "You say we've spoken before, but I don't remember you. How long have they kept me like this?"

"What? No! No! Please, calm. You are not a prisoner. You are a *patient*. The cocoon is a regenerative device. You're almost done with your treatment, but the more still you remain, the easier the process. That's why they kept you sedated."

"'They'? You're not a doctor?"

"No. Fault reflexive. You do not remember me. Please, calm, and I shall begin as if for the first time. I'm Georj Brenna, a historian, specializing in the ancient relic hunters of Keldar Station. I was called from the University when you first awoke. You were pulled from the wreckage of a most spectacular explosion, seen even through the chaos of the Disk, I'm told."

"Explosion?" Suddenly, everything came flooding back. "My ship! Santiago! Is Santiago all right?"

"Santiago was a shipmate?"

"The ship's AI—artificial intelligence. You still have those, right? Did he survive the explosion?"

"I, I do not know..."

"Well, find out!" Dex arched against the restraints and tried to look Brenna square in the eye. Lying still was suddenly torture.

"I've upset you! Fault, reflexive; fault reflexive." Again, he showed his neck. It made Dex think of his gamekeeper father, explaining how in some species, an animal might show its neck to another in the pack to express submission. Is that what Brenna was implying—that Dex should submit?

"Would you stop that?"

The doors opened and he saw two Elomijan nurses, one armed with a device. He thought he recognized it as the one they'd press against his bedding; after which, he'd fall asleep.

"No!" Dex shouted, then took a breath and lay back down. "No, I'll calm down. Just... I need to know about Santiago. Please."

"Patient rest imperative. Georj Brenna vacancy imperative," the nurse said.

Brenna squeezed his shoulder. "I'll find out what I can and return later. Try to rest."

He brushed past the tall, thin nurse, but she remained.

"Status, projective?" she asked, her voice softer with concern. *Are you all right?*

"Fine, reflexive," he growled, though he clenched his jaw to keep from trembling. "Privacy, reflexive, command-request." *I'm fine. Leave me alone.*

He stared at the ceiling until he heard the door shut. They didn't know where Santiago was. They didn't know *what* Santiago was. They didn't know him, either. All his so-called accomplishments, and he wasn't even a blip on a historian's radar. Just another random relic hunter dredged up from the past.

He'd sacrificed everything to catch that Civ B ship. It would have meant a quantum leap in technology for the human race, and wealth and fame for him and his ship. Instead...

"Santiago, my friend. My companion. My rescuer. I'm sorry. I was a stubborn fool, and I am so sorry."

He had not truly cried since he was 14 and he'd broken his leg on a cliff and thought he was going to die. Not for any injury. Not even for Scarlet. But there, in the hospital bed, nearly 600 years from the home he knew, Dex wept.

* * *

Dex stood on a simple green path lined with a thin grove of trees bearing many branches but few leaves. The branches and even the roots stretched out into a starry nothingness. He felt more himself, without the pain, lacking the familiar aches of old age, his mind focused and fresh.

"Am I dreaming or hallucinating?" he groused. "Or did I finally die?"

"Is that any way to ask?" a familiar other-worldly voice responded, and he spun to see Elomij sauntering toward him. She glowed with power and glory, and he felt a new strength in her. Though he mastered his knees and kept them from buckling in her presence, he could not stop from staring in awe.

"You..." He swallowed. "You look good."

She laughed. "I am the goddess of beauty and change. I forgot that for a time while with Hudon; now, I am myself again. Do you approve?"

She moved toward him, somehow swaying while seeming to float. There were things he wanted to ask her, things he needed to tell her, but she breathed upon his neck and his thoughts fled, replaced by the feelings of a young man's body.

She set a hand on his chest, then circled him, dragging her fingers lazily over his chest and back, and where her fingertips trailed, warm tingles flowed, up and down, filling him with dizzying pleasantness.

"You've awakened me, Hunter. Reminded me of who I am. Do you see this road? It is a new people, broken away from the Bloody Road, yet still bearing the gift of my Eye."

The Eye. He'd heard a legend about the Eye… He forced himself to think past her glamour. The Eye… a present to the People. It was supposed to help them grow in wisdom and… something. But it was tainted by jealousy and violence. Because…

"Hudon. He tricked you. Replaced a jewel in the Eye."

"Yes, I know. The People still have it. It makes them more interesting." She finished her circumnavigation and stood smiling before him. Her eyes shone with mischief, adding a youthful quality to her otherworldly beauty.

He squeezed his eyes shut and shook his head against desire.

"Why do you fight, Hunter?"

"What about Hudon?"

"What about him? He is with Corsha. They suit each other."

Death. Something about death. "No, no, that's not good. She's going to kill them all—all the People."

Elomij laughed. "That would be her way."

"You don't understand!" He grabbed her shoulders and shook her. "Not just some of the people at a time. All the People—at once! The entire species. Wiped out in the blink of an eye. Is that what you want? Is that what you would have come of your gift? How can there be change—how can there be growth—when the goddess of death has had her way?"

Her sparkling glory dimmed, and she looked away, pensive. He kept hold of her shoulders, willing her with his mind to listen to him and to do something before it was too late.

Instead, she turned her face toward the green and growing road that expanded slowly before them. She stepped away from his grasp. "Those are Hudon's people now. His choice; his lot. Other concerns await me now, down the path of these People. My people. Perhaps they await the both of us?"

She twisted her head back to him and held out her hand.

Again, he felt a wave of desire, as undeniable and physical as he'd felt in his adolescence. Now, however, instead of embarrassing him as it sometimes had, it brought to mind coffee-colored hair and eyes brilliant with love.

"I can't. I love Scarlet."

"Scarlet is dead, in that otherness you call heaven. Even I cannot change that."

"Then perhaps it's time I join her there."

She tilted her head, curious. "Is that what you wish? To end your adventures?"

"Do you know for a fact that death is not a new adventure?"

"Do you know that it is? You yourself just asked how can change happen if Corsha has had her way."

He couldn't answer. He just knew that life *had* changed after Scarlet's death, and not for the better. Had he been living, or just existing? Was that why he'd clung so tightly to that captured ship, to feel alive again?

Elomij didn't step closer, but did turn fully toward him, one hand still out in invitation. "You need not return to your mortal life. I can offer new adventures."

He didn't trust himself not to reach toward her. His hands fisted under crossed arms. "No. Dead with Scarlet, or alive without;

but not this. You are not my god. I don't belong here."

She smiled. "I think you are more a part of us than you know. Nevertheless, I return you to your life—and I give you a gift."

"I don't want your gifts."

She arched one brow and grinned. "You think I give you the choice to refuse? Remember your place, mortal. Now, return. Sleep. Awaken to my gift."

* * *

Later that day, Brenna opened the door, then tapped on it and approached with mincing steps, his face contorted in an apologetic smile.

"Did you find out what happened to Santiago?" Dex demanded, though the answer was plain on his face.

Brenna pulled the seat closer to the bed. "Unfortunately, it's a little more complicated than that. Bureaucracy, which I understand was quite a tangle even in your time, has not benefited from the Unification, I'm afraid."

"Just give me the short of it."

"The short. Such an anachronistic expression. It went out of style with the improvements in trans-Disc communications, you know, and..."

Dex glared at him, and he shuffled uncomfortably and tried again.

"Yes. Well. There are relic hunters even today; ironically, we are sometimes finding ships of your era, the original relic hunters. I remember the first time I saw one of those early ships..."

"The short!"

"Yes! Yes! The short. The explosion was quite expansive; it drew several hunters to the area. Naturally, they had all taken some of the salvage. You, of course, were the first to return, as you were still alive and in dire need of hospitalization. That was almost six months ago, objective. The other relic hunters returned after that with their finds, which they have sold or are selling, or have sent to their companies for processing. The pieces are scattered across the quadrant by now. It will be a difficult search—but fear not!" He held up his hand to stop Dex from rising against his cocoon. "As the original owner of the ship with the captured ship in tow, you have a right to at least part of the salvage. I have enlisted the assistance of the Rights and Acquisitions Office."

Dex clenched his teeth and made as gracious a thanks as he could, given his disappointment. It was the best he could hope for, he supposed.

Brenna patted his shoulder reassuringly. "Do not despair based on limited information. I hope to have more definitive news by the time you are hatched."

"Hatched?"

"Released, from the cocoon."

"When will that be?" Now that he was awake more often and for longer periods of time, his body had started to complain about the confinement. He'd had a horrid episode of his nose itching; after an irritating half an hour of trying to ignore it, wiggle it away, and trying to scratch it with his teeth, he'd longed for the escape of drugged sleep.

"A day or two. Perhaps a week. I think they are concerned about your mental state."

Dex laughed, an angry, unpleasant sound. "My *mental state* would be much improved if I were neither drugged nor bound to this bed. I want to move, Brenna. I want to pace and move my arms and scratch my vaccing nose!"

He turned his head toward the corner Brenna had been staring at earlier. "You hear me? I'm going to go stir crazy if you leave me like this much longer!"

As if on cue, the door opened, and a tall, broad-shouldered human in a white medical uniform leaned across the threshold.

"I've been waiting to hear that," he said. "Welcome back to life, sir."

Dex scowled. "Why haven't I seen you before?" he accused.

The doctor entered the room and moved to the foot of the bed. Dex had to crane his neck to see him, and the instrumentation around the doctor gave him a reddish haze. Dex blinked.

"Do you remember now? When we were first settling you into the treatment gel, you saw me. Called me Hudon, screamed all sorts of unpleasant things. The staff was quite impressed with your knowledge of Elomij and Hudon."

Dex felt his face flush with embarrassment. "We had some tapes on the *Santiago*," he said. It was true, but not the full story. From the time he and Santiago had captured the Civ B ship and been pulled across the event horizon, he'd had vivid encounters with the alien goddess of change and her consort, the god of war. His battle to survive had been some kind of game between the two. He'd infuriated Hudon with his tenacity and ingenuity as much as by his refusal to bow before the alien gods on their own turf.

He was more than a little proud of himself for that, but that didn't mean he wanted to share his visions of the Bloody Road with the doctor. Especially if his "mental state" was determining how long he needed to stay in the cocoon.

But come to think of it, when was the last time he'd had a memory attack? Granted, he'd only been truly conscious for a day, but even with all his idle time, he never found himself swept up into some past event that relived itself with the vividness of a hallucination.

"I had Blacksone's," he started.

"Past tense. Correct. We've healed you of that. It's still a pernicious disease, even with our advanced medicine. I'll want to monitor you for at least a decade or two to ensure there are no setbacks."

"A decade or two?" Dex snorted. "Doc, if I'm still alive, I'm not sure I'm going to much care. Might even be glad to sit around wallowing in memories while I wait to die." *Especially if those memories involve Scarlet.*

With his face still in shadow, Dex could not see the doctor's expression, but the tilt of his head indicated Dex had said something confusing or stupid. "What?"

Brenna glanced now to the doctor, then answered. "Dex, you don't understand the extent of the damage to your body. Fault reflexive. I was to have prepared you, but yesterday, things did not go as well as planned."

"Just give it to me straight—and Doc, get over here where I can see your face."

The doctor obliged, and Dex was momentarily derailed. While he'd looked human enough in the doorway, and indeed had the stockier build and skin color of a human, he had the facial features and split pupils of an Elomijan.

"Human mother; Elomijan father. But indeed, we are all the People. And you are as well, Dex Hollister. It wasn't just the trauma of the battle, exposure to space, and the Blacksone's you suffered from. Your body had been partially spaghettified."

"Not possible!" The extreme gravity of an event horizon caused simultaneous stretching along one axis of an object while compressing it everywhere else—like stretching dough to make spaghetti. Santiago had been equipped with the strongest shields of their era to protect them. No one and nothing survived spaghettification. Could Santiago's shields have only partially failed? Was that even possible?

Had Elomij saved him?

Dex shook his head. "Ridiculous."

"We thought so as well. Yet there you were, alive but with damage that no one had ever seen before. Even your DNA had been stretched and torn. The body you have is not just your old body healed. You are something very new."

He shivered. "Show me."

The doctor hesitated. "This is why we are concerned with your emotional and psychological state—"

"Show me!"

The doctor must have expected this. He reached into his pocket for a small hand mirror, which he held in front of Dex's face.

Dex stared back at his pale reflection through slit pupils.

Chapter Two

Hudon and the End of the Bloody Road

Hudon and his new consort, Corsha, God-dess of Death, were much suited for each other. She shared in his bloodlust, and they gloried in the fatalities brought on by Hudon's wars. She joined with him in singing their songs, and together they danced to martial ballads. Where their feet trod along the bloody road, brilliant battles ended in equally brilliant deaths. Thus, she fueled Hudon's passions, and her own as well, until in her hunger she cried out for Hudon to give her all their lives.

Now there was among the Eternal Fields a jewel known as Conflict. This was the jewel which Hudon had chipped and hidden a shard of into the Eye that Elomij had given the *people. That small shard had sparked the wars that excited Hudon and Corsha so deeply.*

Upon Corsha's cry, the jewel called Conflict cracked. Its pieces scattered across the Might-Have-Been and fell upon the paths, and from the original jewel leaked a poison, Hubris. The poison took hold of the people. No longer did the glory of combat satisfy them, and their fighting became even more frenetic, their victories more destructive, until one day, the people created the most glorious weapon of all.

When this weapon was activated, the whole of the People of the Bloody Road were destroyed, all at once, in a single aching cry, and their deaths filled the goddess, and her writhing stirred the very fabric of space. When she could stand it no longer, she burst forth across the universe. That is why to this day all things die, for no longer was the goddess of death contained in a single form. She continues to call to all living things, demanding their lives and all they own, all they make and even the very fabric of their worlds. Someday, they will fill her, and all existence will be gone forever.

But while the People of the Bloody Road had been sacrificing themselves to the whims of Hudon and Corsha, Elomij had created a new way, a road of growth and peace, ideas, and cooperation. She brought her people to this road, and there they thrived. They escaped the Alldeath, and it was good.

But when she felt the dispersal of Corsha, which rained even upon her own people and to the beginning of Time, she knew what had happened, and she felt sympathy for her former consort. She left her People to seek him. This is known as the Doldrums, for in this time, the People did not progress, but gave themselves to lethargy and fleeting entertainments.

Elomij found Hudon at the end of the Bloody Road, grieving, diminished without foes to keep him entertained. Her heart ached to comfort him, while at the same time, she feared that if he knew of her People, he would revive the battles of the Bloody Road and ruin her own paths into the future.

So she backtracked along the Bloody Road, following the trail of destruction in reverse until she came to the time of Hudon's angry footprints, when the People had created machines capable of carrying on their battles even after the deaths of their crews. And she breathed upon the manufacturers, and fed their dreams, so that they awoke with *a new plan, and created machines that would fight themselves.*

Then she reached into Corsha's warping of space, spun it with her power, and created a haven free of siren song of the goddess of death. There she placed the machines, but not the People, lest she stir Corsha's desires anew. And when she was done, she presented this new playing field to her consort.

"Look upon this, dear Hudon," she said. "Brilliant battles, logically executed, master-fully enacted, all for your pleasure."

And as he gazed, enraptured once more, she returned home.

"If you say, 'fault, reflexive'..." Dex warned as Brenna entered the hospital room. A week had passed, and still no sign of Santiago. Every day, Brenna came to visit, reporting his failure—though he called it "progress"—and asking Dex questions about his past life. He wanted to know everything, from what it was like growing up on a wildlife preserve to the technology used to communicate through the time dilation to how Dex had courted Scarlet. In return, he explained more about Keldar, the People, and the Elomij.

Their conversations never satisfied either of them. Brenna pushed Dex for more details.

While he relished any conversational aside as if it were a gift, he was always disappointed by what Dex felt were perfectly complete answers. Meanwhile, Dex constantly pulled him back to the topic whenever he went off on a tangent.

"You speak Fusion, but you do not understand how the People communicate!" Brenna had exclaimed in frustration more than once.

"How can I when you're the only one who talks to me?" Dex would snark back. "The doctors only ask me simple questions, and the rest of the staff practically run when I ask them anything."

"They're intimidated," Brenna said. "They think—"

"—that I'm the Huntradex. Yes, I know." It was bad enough he was a six-hundred-year-old relic of the time before Unification. No, his miraculous and unprecedented appearance, combined with his rantings when he was still gravely injured, had somehow earned him the title. He'd managed to learn from the teaching tapes they'd given him that the Huntradex was a kind of harbinger of change, a prophet to announce the coming of the next Hudonite. It didn't help that in his bizarre visions while on the other side of the black hole, Elomij had called him her "Huntradex." He'd thought she was combining "hunter" and "Dex" and being cute about it. It bothered him more than he liked to admit that the word had real meaning he could not have known then.

Regardless, it was making his life difficult. The doctors, at least, came in, checked instruments, and were satisfied with his taciturn answers. They didn't seem to care that he was a living relic or the fabled Huntradex. The nurses and orderlies, however, treated him with disturbing reverence and, now that he was awake, didn't seem interested in talking to him at all. From their timid subservience, they seemed almost afraid of what change he might bring.

Or maybe it's just my winning personality, he thought. He'd been too many years alone with only his AI and the occasional fellow relic hunter to talk to. He'd enjoy the quiet and privacy. Now, he had neither for longer than a few hours. But he also had no one aside from Brenna to break up the long drudge of his waking hours.

The teaching tapes, basic orientation for a relic hunter gone too long in the Disk, covered essential information he needed to adapt to this new age, but it was too basic to fire his intellect while at the same time leaving gaps that anyone who had lived in the last century could fill in. Like how to carry on a polite conversation.

Brenna was his only source for filling in the gaps, but he was hungry for every detail of Dex's era. Dex hadn't cared who the leaders of the nearby worlds were. He knew about some of the religions, but other than a simple Christian wedding ceremony to please Scarlet's family, he hadn't practiced. Brenna had once subjected him to an hour of looking at old images, trying to attach names to some of the faces, and Dex realized that even if he'd known them and spoken to them, his eyes had been so bad by then he probably wouldn't be able to recognize them.

Worst of all, however, it had made him realize he was having a harder time remembering Scarlet's face. He hadn't expected that. Only months ago, subjective to himself, memories would ambush him with such intensity that he would re-live them to the exclusion of all else. Now, he could barely pull up the image of her smile.

In all, it had left him tired, restless, and spoiling for a fight. He tried to pour his energy into learning to use his new body, and badgering Brenna about Santiago. Usually, that meant the historian would show his neck and

say. "Fault reflexive," a saying Dex was growing to loathe.

Today, however, Georj Brenna greeted
him with a smile.

"No. I have good news! We were able to
secure your rights to the spacesuit in which
we found you."

"My *spacesuit*? What about my *ship*?"

Brenna held up his hands in what was still
the gesture for *let me speak*. "Patience. This is
an important step. With these rights, you now
have income: royalties in return for permis-
sion to display and study of your property.
And I have published the first of our inter-
views, for which, you receive a portion of the
profits. Using that, I have secured an investigator well-versed in cases like this–"

"Like mine?" Just how many hundreds-
years-old relic hunters did they deal with on
Keldar?

If Brenna heard the skepticism in Dex's
voice, he didn't notice. "Oh, yes. After all, the
People—human, then Elomij—have been ex-
ploring the Disk for centuries now. Ships are
lost, but families remain. When the ships are
found again, the progeny deserve the fruits of
their ancestors' courage and hard work, don't
you agree? There are many investigators, but

I have secured for you Dolon, the best of her kind."

Dex interrupted again. "So, there have been others that have crossed back from the event horizon?"

"She... What?" Brenna's face drained. "You say...you were on the other side? And you *came back*?"

Dex huffed and banged his head against the pillow. Surely, he'd mentioned it? But no, of all the questions Brenna had asked, he never inquired about what had caused Dex to be discovered in the accretion disk 600 years in his own future. "What do you think destroyed my ship?"

"I thought... Your ship had been damaged, and you'd been stuck in a swarl, or maybe a clockwork of swarls, unable to escape, the gravity slowly tearing your ship apart until got too close to the event horizon and spaghettified. No one has said any different to me."

Dex snorted. "Nothing in the Disk could have done that. Not to me. Not to the *Santiago*."

"No wonder they think you are the Huntradex. To return from the land swallowed by Corsha, Goddess of Death."

"Never mind the mythology, please. Tell me about this investigator. The short version."

"Yes, of course." Brenna cleared his throat as if dispelling the barrage of questions he now had thanks to Dex's revelation. Dex knew they'd come later, but at least the historian was more skilled at reading his moods and knew to wait.

"The investigator. Dolon Scenza. Very experienced in tracking unusual artifacts. Mostly works for collectors and such, but she was most excited to take your case. She also has a license in Rights Acquisition and Securing, so should she find your AI, Santiago, she'll be able to negotiate for his release to you." Now he stopped and grimaced. "Assuming, of course, that there's anything left to secure."

Dex glared at the ceiling, digesting this information. "There will be. There has to be. After all, I survived, and Santiago would make sure he was around to remind me of the fact. So, you've discussed this with her? Does she have any idea how long this will take?"

Georj shook his head. "I spoke to her less than an hour ago. I thought you would like the news right away. She will come to you when she has something."

Dolon Scenza visited Dex two days after his hatching, what they called releasing him from the regenerative cocoon. He was standing, legs in braces, arms in crutches and a brace on his back to support him as he shuffled across the room, re-teaching his body to walk. He'd waved her in impatiently, nearly toppling as he did so. She did not move to catch him, but leaned against the wall, arms crossed, out of his way, watching intently as he caught his own balance and made a careful turn back toward the bed. She said, "Nonexistent time viewing ambulatory relic six centuries aged."

Never seen a six hundred-year-old relic walk before. Gradually, the need to translate in his head was fading, and his ability to speak Fusion naturally grew. He said something rude in return.

Scenza laughed. "It was a compliment, old timer. To your doctors and you." The slits of her pupils widened, a sign he'd learned from the teaching tapes implied attraction.

He wasn't sure how to react to that. His new body, young as well as healthy, found her attractive as well. But his mind, eighty-nine years aged and six hundred out of its time, didn't know how to process that. He wasn't sure he wanted to. Without the Blacksone's to keep Scarlet immediate to his mind, he'd found himself grieving all over again, something he did quietly lest the doctors decide he needed sedating and more time in the cocoon.

Learn to walk first. Then I can run, or whatever. He set his site on his target—the closet at the end of the room—and urged his foot forward. The braces assisting his strength and balance whirred. The louder the whine, the more work they were doing. When he'd first started, they'd assailed his ears with their screeching; now they made a rumbling purr.

"Any news on my ship?" he asked with a grunt.

She reached into the bag slung over her shoulder. As she spoke, she tossed items onto his bed. "Bills of sale for hull parts of ancient human composites, a repair bot, still in amazing condition, currently on display at the Kaltinian Institute—I'm securing your share of the profits from those—and..." She held up a silvery package and squinted at the writing on the label. "A six-hundred-year-old bag of something called daw-slu."

"*Dawlsu!* Is it still fresh?" He was so sick of hospital food! The braces squealed as he changed direction toward her.

"It might have been three months ago when you first crossed back into this universe, but it's been sitting in a cargo bay all this time, along with a bunch of detritus from other runs no one knows what to do with. The seal seems compromised."

She tossed him the pack. He fumbled to catch it—causing the braces on his arms to whine—and ripped it open. His nose wrinkled at the spoiled smell. "Vac!"

"Apparently not, then. Fault reflexive, negative. If I'd been hired earlier, I might have been able to find and preserve it for you."

"Not my fault." Yeah, yeah. "Next time I'm hunting the Disk, I'll put you on retainer."

"Honesty verified? Is that what you plan to do?"

"Definitive unverified, reflexive. I can't think that far yet. Right now, I'm concentrating on walking and finding my AI." He looked at her with narrowed eyes, a human gesture that still worked with his new face.

She shrugged and pushed herself off the wall. "For ambulation and independence, progress rapid suspected reflexive. I know determination when I see it."

She thinks I'll be recovered soon. Well, the docs agree there. "And Santiago?"

"If he's still around, I'll find him." She crossed her wrists, palms up, in the Elomijan farewell, but did not linger for him to cross his own wrists and touch her fingers. It would have been too hard with the braces.

After she left, he contemplated the bag of dawlsu still in his grip, then tossed it into the biowaste can with a rueful sigh. Soon enough, he'd find out what the People on station ate. First, he had to learn to walk. He straightened and concentrated on getting to the door with a minimum of mechanical grumble.

* * *

"I told you, I don't know," Dex said to Brenna again. "She never told me. Now, drop it."

Dex gripped the edges of his mattress, lest he give into the urge to leap off the bed and start pacing. After the day he'd had in physical therapy, he'd probably end up flat on his face, and he'd already had enough frustration and humiliation for the day. It hadn't helped that the therapist, a substitute and new, had reacted with profuse "fault, reflexive"s and barings of his neck. Dex had been very tempted to swipe at the exposed skin just to teach him a lesson, except that he'd probably take it as some kind of curse by the "mighty Huntradex."

Brenna had passed the point of fawning, but even after three weeks, he didn't persist in his questions or in his demand for encyclopedic answers. Today, his persistence seemed to speak like accusations of failure.

"Please, think, Dex. Molly must have told you how she got the job with the Relic Hunter's Union. Any detail might open up more memories."

"How may times do I have to say it? Scarlet died. Molly wanted time alone. I left her on Keldar while I did a run. I came back, she had the job. We moved on."

"And that was enough for you, that she had a job? You said she was like a daughter."

"Don't," Dex warned. "Do not put your cultural norms on my past. She had moved on. That's what children and apprentices do. I was proud. It was enough."

Brenna frowned at his notes. "To this day, I still spend many enjoyable hours sharing my triumphs with my parents. Why, when I was granted sabbatical to come here and study you..."

Oh, not another long story about an even longer conversation with his parents. "Get out!"

"...and my mother reminded me how I would often record the conversations with my grandfather. 'The way you dive into the past; it is how you have been kissed by Elomij'... What?"

"Get. Out. It's only two words. Would it be more understandable if I spent half an hour describing exactly how you should leave? Go!"

Brenna sighed and tapped off the recording device on his wrist. He stood.

"I'll be back tomorrow."

Dex couldn't tell if he'd meant it as a promise or a threat. He replied by laying back and staring at the ceiling.

Outside, he heard Brenna speaking in quiet tones to someone. If he was ratting him out to the doctors...

But a few minutes later, Dolon, not a nurse, walked through his door. He kept brooding at the ceiling.

She frowned down at him. "Rise, request-imperative. While this behavior may have been acceptable to humans of your era, it borders on psychological disorder now."

"Do you have word about my ship?"

She crossed her arms and waited silently. With a sigh, he sat up.

She ignored his scowl. "Come, let us walk to the atrium, where the surroundings are more pleasant."

He didn't want to walk. Or more to the point, he didn't want to stumble. But he did feel like spring wound too tight. He needed to move. And she was right; the view in the atrium was far better than his hospital room, even with most of the medical equipment gone or tucked aside.

Besides, even in the mood he was in, Dolon was welcome company. She asked direct questions and was fine with plain answers. She understood the quick comeback. Here was someone he could banter with. She was also content to wait in silence as he worked out his own thoughts.

With a shrug of agreement, he motioned for her to hand him his braces. They made their way down the hall, moving more slowly than his angry mood wanted, but at a speed his legs could handle. As they walked, she gave him a succinct report of the artifacts she'd found that could be credited in whole or part to him, his growing financial nest egg of royalties, the lead she was pursuing on Santiago. By the time she'd finished, they'd made a full circuit of the atrium and his mood had calmed.

"Why aren't the others like you?" he asked after they found seats under a shimmering tree and stared silently out the clear rooftop at the stars.

"I have spent my life among relic hunters," she said. "I understand how they speak."

"I speak Fusion just fine," he grumped.

"Affirmation, projective. However, do not confuse language with how you speak. The People communicate in story and reflexive experience. They savor the fullness of detail as you once savored the spice of dawlsu. Relic hunters have a more telegraphic style. It makes sense; when dealing with time dilation, it's important to come to the point quickly. When you are fully hale, I will introduce to you some of my regular clients.

"You, however, take brevity to a level unseen in centuries. You are direct, succinct, projective. No one of the People would presume to ask a question as you do, even relic hunters. Your answers are insulting in their simplicity, just like you complain some of the training tapes are. And your impatience is often construed as judgmental and rude."

He blinked, completely taken aback. "Please, don't go easy on me."

Scarlet would have laughed to diffuse the tension. Dolon raised a brow and replied with mild seriousness. "I do not because if I did, you would not respect me. And do not assume that I speak to anyone else the way I speak with you, Dex Hollister. One of my talents is understanding how a client thinks and adapting accordingly. In that way, I am kissed by Elomij herself. However, for all that my people embrace change, we have our limits."

"And I'm too much?" He found himself grinning. He liked her frank style.

She nodded. "It does not help that some have it in their minds that you are the Huntradex."

He sighed. There it was again. "Do you believe that?"

She looked him over. He wondered what she saw. In the dim light of the Atrium, he could not see her eyes well enough to know if they shone with attraction, judgement, or annoyance. Her expression was neutral. Finally, she returned to stargazing.

"It remains to be seen. There have been many Huntradexes since the creation of the People of Flomij, and many false ones as well. The Huntradex becomes known by the changes that follow him or her. We're talking societal changes. Usually, the Huntradex is followed by the Hudonite who is the instrument of change."

"Like Brenna?"

She snickered, more in surprise at the thought than in humor. "That would be a stretch of the imagination. Nor would it be me. Sometimes, there is no Hudonite, and those are dangerous times. Your behavior when delirious and your ability to speak and understand a language that did not develop until almost a century after your disappearance indicates you are gods-kissed. So, for all that you deserve honor for that and respect as a patient, the new behaviors you demonstrate are not the behaviors we wish to embrace. The politest way they can handle that is by limiting their exposure to you."

"Great," he grumbled. "So, it is my personality."

He glared at the stars, but a moment later, he heard Dolon snort. He turned to see her staring at him, her face twisted with mirth she fought to contain. Soon, he, too, chuckled, and as if a dam had been opened, they began to laugh outright. It felt good.

That evening when the nurse came in to check his vitals, he followed Dolon's advice and launched uninvited into the story of his and Dolon's conversation in the atrium. As she had instructed, he tried to recall every detail and assign it significance. He felt like an idiot, but when he'd run out of things to say and finally ended with a lame, "It was an interesting evening," the nurse thanked him with genuine warmth as she bid him goodnight. Even better, she seemed just a bit more comfortable.

Dolon, meanwhile, shared her side of the story with the staff, and with Georj Brenna. Dex suspected that she also reminded them how much had changed since he'd been a part of the real-time world. As the weeks passed, they grew more comfortable around him, and even started to give suggestions and answer questions.

Dex and Brenna also reached a kind of conversational compromise, where Brenna learned to curb his monologues to 90 seconds or less while Dex struggled to increase his explanations to seven facts or more.

Overall, it was an improvement, though not a perfect solution.

"The thing is," Brenna said after the librarian had dropped off more tapes and left with the usual bowings, "the Elomijans take their religion very seriously. When you called Dr. Zinda 'Hudon,' I think half the staff thought that they'd be struck dead as you and Hudon engaged in epic battle."

"I was delirious." Dex sighed. Would he ever tell anyone about the hallucinations he'd had while in the black hole? He'd seen Elomij, though she'd looked human enough, and her husband Hudon. They'd called him Hunter Dex. Not far from Huntradex. Could any of it have been real, and the name simply shifted linguistically over the centuries?

He rubbed his temples with one hand, as if that would protect him from this insanity. "I'd been listening to the legends; and the Blacksone's, it does things to your memory. You start reliving things—even stories."

"They're more than stories, Dex. This is their *religion*. I may not believe. You may not believe, but they do—and many believe you are the Huntradex."

Dex sighed. "How do I get them to stop?"

"Only time can do that. The Huntradex emerges once every several generations when the people have become stagnant and need to be pushed along the path. They are the harbingers of change, if not the change itself. You may yet be a Huntradex. You have been through so much. I wish to write a biography of you if you will permit it. But after the treatise on pre-Unity culture. Things I've taught for years as established fact, you've told me are not only different but outright wrong. You do not realize how much misinformation is out there. Even the way we look at family dynamics."

"Fault reflexive, negative." Dex toyed with his food. A few more tests, a few more days, then he'd be free of the walls of the hospital complex. And what would he do then? No skills except navigating the Disk; his physics knowledge centuries out of date, so that even the most basic concepts of the age jarred around his mind and refused to take root. No place to go once he did get released. Brenna had suggested he go on the lecture circuit, but the idea of sharing his life story to hundreds of strangers—or worse, Elomijan strangers—made him want to re-cross the event horizon. At least the infernal machines he'd battled within the black hole didn't pepper him with questions.

Maybe I should go home, find out if the parkland's still there. Return to my roots. Wouldn't Dad have gotten a thrill from that?

He missed what Brenna was saying. "Pardon?"

"I said, 'credit projective emphatic.' You have no idea how your presence has energized me—energized all who have studied this area of history. You've given me new life as definitively as the doctors have given you new life."

He raised his glass. "What's a relic for?"

Even with things getting better, Dolon's visits were still the highlight of the day, even though she didn't have any news about

Santiago. At least she seemed to understand his quandary better than anyone.

"I've been working on some projections," she told him as she sat on his bed and watched him working the arm weights, her legs swinging in time to the motions of his exercise. She wore a split skirt that stopped at her knees. Elomij had a layer of short fur on their legs and feet, and he found himself wondering if it felt as silky as it looked.

"I've made some estimates based on your percentages of the profits from relics I've found, as well as one with projections based on what I think I can find. If you live moderately, the profits you'll have in the next year should last you ten. Not bad for a bunch of scrap."

Dex huffed, as much from disgust as effort against the weights. "If I'd have brought that ship back intact, Santiago and I'd have been set for life—this life, even."

He pulled the weight up too quickly, not paying attention to his posture. His shoulder crawled with sudden heat, and he dropped the weight in surprise. It fell to the floor with a plop. He was still getting used to the messages of his alien nerves. Who knew pain could feel so different?

Dolon hopped off the bed and moved behind him, rubbing his shoulder. He could feel each of her fingers digging into four pressure points. It hurt at first, then the tension released, and he could breathe more easily.

"I'll find him," she promised. "And when I find him, I'll have his condition evaluated and get an estimate on repair if possible."

Her words, as confident as her touch, relaxed his fears. "It's possible. You don't know Santiago. Most versatile piece of programming ever written encased in hardware that was years ahead of its time. He's a survivor."

"Comparison projective?"

He laughed. "Comparison reflexive, verified. Yeah, like me. You'll like him."

"And what will you do when you find him? Install him into a new ship?"

He paused. Dolon had bought him time. Time to acclimate, to learn a new trade—or maybe, with Santiago's help, begin again with his old one. Time to figure out what he wanted to do with this bizarre new second life he'd been given.

Humans had their own myths. One was about creatures with nine lives. What did they do with their new beginnings? He wished one were around to ask.

"Perhaps we should race?" Dolon suggested. "I shall pit my ability to find your AI against your ability to conquer your new body and be released from the hospital. Competition is part of the Elomijan way."

Had Dolon mistaken his silence for doubt in her abilities? He opened his mouth to apologize but stopped. Scarlet used to pout if he underestimated her. And if—when, usually when—she'd proven him wrong; she would refuse his apology. Dolon instead had issued a challenge. He liked it. "Humans, at least in my time, competed for prizes. What do I get if I win?"

Her bottom lip jutted in an Elomijan expression of thought. "Dinner, and escort and guide to the more interesting areas of the station, including activities the doctor might not approve of?"

Was she coming on to him? Then again, he thought about the staid, cautious physician. Probably anything beyond a short walk was not on the approved list. "And if you win?"

"Dinner, and a night on the station arm-in-arm with a six-century legend."

He grinned. "Including activities not medically approved?"

"Definitive unverified reflexive if they are medically approved—merely not Doctor Zinda's preference."

Her pupils widened and contracted—an Elomijan wink—and he felt his eyes repeat the gesture. The alien sensation left him pleasantly dizzy.

He was too embarrassed to ask the librarian, so when Brenna came the next afternoon for their discussions, he asked him to bring some tapes on Elomijan courtship.

CHAPTER THREE

As he'd grown more personable with the staff, they'd grown more interested in helping with his acclimation. One of the orderlies started bringing him "adventures"—two-dimensional video dramas. No one had thought about it as a way to teach him. Apparently, the People were generally too social to embrace such passive entertainment. Cej, the orderly, only thought of it when Dex told him a story of how Scarlet had insisted they eat dawlsu with a spoon and fork after seeing it on a holo.

The adventures were so long and plot so slow, he'd set them aside, but after Dolon's warning, he forced himself to watch the one about a small community within a planetary city. He gritted his teeth and made notes on the interactions, then asked Cej about the writing—how much rang true and how much was played out for dramatic effect. He found himself enjoying those conversations, and for the first time laughed with another Elomijan aside from Dolon.

Even so, just as with his physical training, his social training seemed to be two steps forward, one back.

Dolon sat across from him at the table of his new room. They'd set it up specifically so he could get used to the furniture of the century, which tended to encourage reclining and sitting with legs tucked up instead of the straight seats that had been the standard for his previous life. Tables, too, were odd: narrow horseshoe-shaped things. Plates and even bowls were likewise long and narrow. Soup bowls had curved lips; the Elomijan sipped rather than spooned. At least there was a spork.

At the moment, Dex was stabbing his meat with the spork while Dolon leaned back and glared at him with crossed arms and narrow eyes. For humans of his time, that would have signaled that she was backing off and giving him a chance to think about the lecture she'd just delivered. For the People—Elomijan and modern humans—it meant she was just getting started.

"I am thinking you don't want to win our bet at all. You will not be released from the hospital until you can show at least some basic Elomijan manners, and the more time I spend teaching you, the less time I have to concentrate on finding your Santiago."

"Then why are you taking the time?" he growled. He sounded like a surly teenager; he knew. It had been so long ago, but he thought he felt like an adolescent, too. Was this new body still in puberty? That was a disturbing thought.

He turned his mind back to Dolon's words. She'd been saying something about his health and independence being more important than finding an ancient computer.

"Do not misunderstand me, Dex Hollister. I do not diminish the innate importance of Santiago nor its importance to you. If anything, that I do should underscore the value I, and the people here, place on your recovery. But you continue to be rude, and today, you made a nurse cry—a nurse who was trying to brief you on your progress and release schedule."

"She did, and when I told her I understood, she launched into yet another version of the same story."

"Dex, you have to give people time to repeat themselves. She was trying to share a deeply personal story in hopes it might motivate you further."

"I am motivated!"

"The fact that we are having this conversation would indicate otherwise."

She sounded so much like Santiago in that moment, Dex found himself grinning despite his annoyance. "Okay. Point taken. But she did share it. Twice."

"She only shared it twice. When an Elomij shares something she considers important, she will say it a third time—four or more, if she is passionate. Repetition assigns impact. Repetition is an invitation to open yourself in return. Likewise, a single acknowledgement is a too-casual recognition that the person has spoken—like how you say, 'uh-huh' when you are clearly distracted."

Had he done that in this conversation? That used to drive Scarlet nuts, too. "Okay. I get it."

"Again, repetition is an important signal. To acknowledge twice is show respect."

"Okay."

She pressed on. "To acknowledge a third time shows you understand the importance of what the person is saying."

"All right! I get it!"

"...perhaps without the annoyed tone...?"

He took a deep breath and released it. He replied slowly, considering his words as he went. "Okay. You are correct. I have a lot to learn still. Is there a learning tape about apologizing? Because I've not seen it, and you're right. Kalin deserves an apology. I appreciate you correcting me when...what?"

Dolon's chin quivered in that way he'd learned meant she was fighting back a laugh. "That was so awkward. But well intentioned. I think something similar would work sufficiently for Kalin as well. However, we shall work on this skill. Have you thoroughly mutilated your meat, or do you wish to 'tenderize' it some more?"

"You know I think the meat is too tough." But he smirked, anyway. The steak was a bulbous landscape of divots.

"Your teeth are sharper now. Not as sharp as your tongue..."

He raised a brow. It felt odd to his new face, but the expression came naturally to his brain. "Or my wits?"

Now, she leaned forward and looked directly into his eyes. He liked it. "I do not believe your wits have ever been less than razor sharp."

"You're right. And I've never backed down from a challenge. That's how I'm alive, and I would share that story if you wish. And with you teaching me, I will learn proper Elomijan manners—beginning with the much-needed apology to Kalin."

Dolon smiled. "Much better! And I do wish. Tell me more about the exploits of Dex and Santiago."

"You realize you're going to lose this competition?" he teased.

She raised a brow in perfect imitation of his earlier move. "Do not presume. I do have another lead, but I cannot discuss it yet. However, should it not lead me to the path of Santiago's journeying, it matters little. Win or lose, I enjoy your company. I bet wisely."

"So, you did. It seems your wits are sharp as well."

"Was there a doubt, Dex Hollister?"

* * *

Dolon's lead did not pan out as expected. Dex won the competition and his freedom from the hospital. Yet, as he stood in front of the bathroom mirror and pulled on the long wine-colored tunic Georj had brought him, strange, slitted eyes stared back at him and belied the hollowness of his victory. No Santiago. No ship. No career, no current skills... No direction.

You have finances for a decade, he reminded himself. Time enough to start over again. You have plenty of possibilities.

But did he? Even as a child, he'd known what he wanted. What did he want now?

He shook himself to expel the gloom and hastened to attach the belt and smooth the tunic over the split skirt that was the fashion for both genders. He wondered if he had the legs to pull it off. He'd never had hairy legs as a human and now, he had a literal pelt. They'd taught him basic care, but did the People on Keldar do anything special with their fur?

He played a little with his belt and the tuck of the tunic over it, trying to get it to look like Davil's in *Long Path of the Gods-kissed*, and feeling completely stupid as he did so.

He laughed at himself. When was the last time he'd cared about how he looked? Probably about the time Scarlet stopped turning heads whenever they went to the station.

He grinned at her memory. Not that she ever stopped being a woman worth pursuing. But it had been nice to be comfortable with each other, to relax into the respect age and success had brought them. There was something to be said for growing old together. Much as he enjoyed the strength and youth of this new body, that was something else he'd lost, too.

He paused, probing the thought the way one poked at a bruise. It did ache still, but not with the intensity it had the first time he'd awakened to find himself in a world without Scarlet. How much of that healing was due to his new body, he wondered? For 20 years, the Blacksone's had not let him get past the memories of her smile, her laugh, her touch. Her death. Now, at last, he could move on.

Moving on. He didn't know he could feel so excited and so guilty at the same time.

The chime rang, and he shook off his introspective mood. New body, new life, new possibilities. And new friends. He hadn't made friends easily even in his old life, but at least here there were a couple of people he could depend on. "Come in, Georj. What do you think?"

Georj eyed him critically. "The belt buckle needs to face the other way—unless you've decided to take a vow of celibacy?"

Had Davil been celibate in that movie? That changed a couple of things. Damn it, he might have to rewatch it now.

More immediately, however, his fashion *faux pas* could make his date with Dolon awkward—if it were a date and not just two friends having dinner. He'd learned from watching *Small Town in the City* that the People, especially the Elomij, were naturally flirtatious, and Cej had confirmed it, though he said he'd never noticed until Dex mentioned it.

"Think I'll keep my options open." He rebuckled it. Then he noticed the direction of Georj's buckle. "Projective...?"

Georj nodded. "After my wife died, I realized there'd be no one else. A story I am glad to share another time. Perhaps after I return from the University. I regret I must return tomorrow evening. There has been so much excitement about the articles, I've been invited to share a full accounting—and you know the People..."

"The more personal, the better," Dex concluded.

Georj nodded. "But as for celibacy: It's a celebrated choice, now—not like in your time, I believe?"

Dex shrugged. Georj knew the answer—he'd asked often enough—but it was just another custom of the People never to miss a chance to invite conversation. "We never really talked about sex, much. We certainly didn't wear it on our belts. What you did was your own business, and people kept it that way."

"I see. Group fault reflexive. The custom of the belts is a centuries-long tradition, along with other small fashion signals. It predates even the oldest relic hunter—present company excepted. We did not think to teach this to you. There are nuances to the wear of the belt, as with so many things about the People, but for now, just remember: to the right; you are open to the right companion. To the left, you have left such attachments behind."

Dex waited, but when he said nothing else, asked, "That's it? No follow-up questions, no request for some long, involved story from my era that loosely relates to clothing?"

Georj grinned, embarrassed. "You've been very patient with me, and I don't know that I can ever fully express my gratitude. However, today isn't about your past. It's about your future, is it not? And I know, if it were me, I'd rather have a friend than a researcher at my side."

Dex gave him a smile and a nod but didn't trust himself to say anything more as they left the room. Maybe he didn't have much, but he did have friends, and that was as good a place as any to start.

Once to the exit level, however, his misgivings returned, especially when the lift doors opened and he found the route to the door lined with the staff, all with heads bowed and arms crossed with palms up. As the lift door opened, they fell into a squat that combined curtsey and kneel.

"Is this a Huntradex thing? Is it going to be like this everywhere I go?" he muttered to Georj. Last night, he'd reread the legends of the first Huntradex, a mortal spirit who visited the Bloody Road, was tested by Hudon, and spoke the prophesies to Elomij that caused her to lead the People away from their destructive path. Elomij had invited the Huntradex to join her in her stroll along the Growing Road, but he had refused. She'd sent him away into the Might-Have-Been, knowing he'd return when she needed another push to care for her People. Then, she would send a Hudonite, named for her lover, to act as agent of change.

Save the Hudonite part, the tales bore an uncanny similarity to the hallucinations he'd had while inside the black hole, but he could not remember now if Santiago had played those legends while he'd been working to fix the ship and escape the black hole. He must have. He had to have. But the fact that he did not know for sure gave him an itch between the shoulder blades, the Elomijan equivalent of the hair standing up on the back of a human neck.

He hadn't told anyone about those hallucinations. Yet here they were, bowing...

"I thought we were past this. Can't you tell them I'm not who they think I am?"

"Aren't you?" Georj said, but this time, humor teased at his voice. "It is written that the Huntradex fought a great battle against jealous Hudon, deep within the stirrings of Corsha, the goddess of death, and in the last moment of despair, broke free of her spell and returned to the Growing Way. Sounds close enough to me, and I'm not even a believer. But don't worry. Hospitals have strict confidentiality about their patients. Outside this hospital, you are just another of the People.

"But this?" Georj gestured to the people lined up like an honor guard. "This is because you are a good man, Dex, who has overcome astronomical odds to survive. You have worked hard for your recovery, and not just of body, but mind and soul. This is to pay homage to who you were and who you are now."

"All right, then." He straightened his shoulders and stepped down the line, thanking each of the Elomijans in turn—for a cool hand when he was feverish, for help eating a meal when he was weak, for assisting him with the braces when he was too tired to move... For being patient when he was not.

He brushed the fingertips offered, a traditional farewell blessing, and saw several eyes tearing. He found himself clearing his throat more than once against emotions he hadn't thought he'd feel.

For four months, he'd suffered, ranted, moped, studied, and trained, but only now did he give any thought to all the work these people had done to put him back together.

Dr. Zinda waited at the door. He held out his fingertips.

Dex brushed them, and then took his hand, human style, and clasped him in a brief hug. "Thank you," he said. "You've..." He paused as his voice caught. "You've given me a second life."

"Use it well. Seek the beauty of your new life. For what are the People if not change?"

Dex nodded against the man's shoulder, then pushed away and walked through the doors without looking back.

The area in front of the hospital was a large, open bubble, with several walkways jutting from the entrance like spokes on a wheel, and two tram lines that stopped before the main entrance. There was a park area with benches and beautiful arching trees that provided shade against the artificial lights. They swayed with subtle motion against a breeze that did not exist. The silvery branches bore leaves that shifted through the color spectrum throughout the day. He'd seen them from the windows during his promenades around the hospital. He'd never been able to guess if they were actual, organic, growing plants or a fabulous sculpture, and Dolon had playfully refused to tell him. Now, with no idea where he should be going, he headed to the nearest one to satisfy his own curiosity.

Georj hurried and caught his elbow just as he'd reached out to a branch.

"I wouldn't do that. Each of those leaves costs about a month of my salary."

Dex jerked his hand back. "So, they're artificial?"

"Yes, and no." Georj steered him through the park to the tunnel on the far side and to the right. "They are real in that they perform much the same functions of living plants—converting carbon dioxide to oxygen, for example—but they have machines built into their fibers that govern their growth, coloration, and the like. I only know what I learned in early schooling, I'm afraid. I've never been much for botany."

The pedestrian traffic made the tunnel feel cramped after the openness of the park, even though it was wider than the corridors of the hospital. Only a few people hurried on their way, twisting shoulders and murmuring apologies as they pushed around small knots of chatters. More often, people meandered, pausing to greet each other and share some gossip. People would break off conversations with a nod and brushing of fingertips, only to start up a new conversation a few feet further along their way.

Dex and Georj strolled, arms linked in Elomijan fashion, at a steady, leisurely pace, but he couldn't help feeling he was intruding on a party composed of scores of close-knit friends.

"Another difference between our times." Georj leaned toward him to whisper. "Always plan extra time for conversations when going anywhere. And the more familiar your route, the more time you should allot. The People are very social. However, they will respect your pace if you are in a hurry."

Of course, Georj had warned him of this, as had Dolon, and even some of the staff. And Dex had picked it up from the teaching tapes and the adventures he'd watched. Nonetheless, he did not respond with an impatient "I know." Even if it was still his first impulse. Besides, the reality of it was a little disconcerting.

He looked for a way to acknowledge Georj's words without simply parroting them back.

"It's... interesting to see it first-hand. I'm afraid it will take some getting used to. This is not the way we did things in my time. So, are we hurrying?" He'd noticed a few people nod to Georj, but none attempted to intercept them and engage them in conversation.

"They know I am bringing a friend to his new home after a long and disorienting hospital stay. This may be the only uninterrupted walk you ever get. However, I should orient you." With that, he started to explain which turns would take Dex to the commissary, gym, shopping, and entertainment areas. He also pointed out the "red light" district. "Called the 'Pleasure Paths,'" he explained, "Although I would not recommend a foray there unless you plan to discard your belt altogether."

A voice behind them said, "It is not worth it, friends possessive reflexive anticipatory! Free advice from one who clawed his way out of the hedonistic singularity."

They paused and turned to see a young Elomijan man, his eyes the same bright green as his tunic, belted to indicate celibacy, the hair of his legs dyed to match the swirling colors of the Disk. In fact, the colors themselves did swirl. For a moment Dex was back on the *Santiago*, looking at a holographic display of the accretion disk, tracing a general path around a swarl and directing Santiago to perfect the route.

It was the most vivid memory he'd had since waking in this new world. Not Blacksone's-level, but enough to cause a clutch in his heart.

The man caught Dex staring, and his smile grew. "A souvenir of wild youth. The injections were painful, and even now it disturbs me how much pleasure I found in that. Still, they are a welcome conversation piece."

"I know that clockwork," Dex found himself saying. He dragged himself into the present enough to point to a spot below the man's right knee, where the fur rippled in a series of interlocked swarls. "It's in the Zone."

"Kay-Serani-Five—a favorite of mine. Even today, we find the best relics there. But I have interrupted your journey! Fault reflexive, mercy projective requested. I am Serani, named for the clockwork we both admire. We navigate the same path. May I join you?"

Dex shrugged, his initial shock past, leaving a new determination to find his AI and friend. To do that, he needed to adapt to this world, and quickly. Might as well get some practice in conversation with a stranger.

Seeing Dex's assent, Georj invited Serani to join them. The process took three times longer than Dex could have imagined. If that was normal, Dex had seriously underestimated how much his friend had held back in their conversations at the hospital.

With a joyful thanks, Serani threaded his arm through Dex's. Even with the wide corridor, they took up a lot of space, yet both Brenna and Serani wound their way through the crowd with ease, almost instinctively knowing who should take the lead when.

"So how is it you know Kay-Serani-Five, and by so archaic a name? I've heard it called 'The Zone' only by the oldest of hunters, who said they heard it from their fathers. Are you a hunter whose journey into the Disk led him well off the path of his own time?"

Dex nodded. "Independent ship's captain. Now without a ship." Admitting it was like a knife piercing his heart. He knew he should say more, but walking through the corridors, healthy and free, made the loss more vivid. "Perhaps we can share the story another time," he managed to say through the catch in his throat.

Serani twisted to let someone pass, greeting him warmly as he did, and then returned his attention to Dex with a more serious expression. "I understand. Condolences and shared grieving. Ship's navigator, reflexive. Unemployed. Wish, projective, the story? Perhaps its telling may distract you from your own pain."

At Brenna's encouragement and Dex's less enthusiastic agreement, Serani started into his tale, going to the very beginning, with his awakened from a drugged orgy feeling completely alone and unfulfilled, and before he had realized what he was doing, had fled from the emptiness out of the Pleasure Paths and to the docks.

"Many an hour I stood there, my friends, gazing upon the ships and thinking my life was as empty and lifeless as their holds. Yet, already I was longing to return and lose myself in a singularity of decadence."

"Uh-huh."

Georj nudged Dex a little with his elbow.

Dex tried again. "To fall back on old ways is a strong temptation. An understandable one. Yet, you are here telling us this story." He hoped his smile looked encouraging and not strained. Serani had already been talking for more than five minutes and two long corridors and he'd not even gotten to his adventure of looking for a job.

When Molly had joined the Hunter's Union and gotten a job on the Pig, she'd simply shown up on the *Santiago* in uniform and said, "So?" Dex had hugged her, said he was proud, and that had been it.

He pulled his attention back to Serani's acknowledgement of his acknowledgement.

"...quite perceptive, my newfound friend! No, I decided my salvation lay in getting as far from, as you called it, temptation, as possible. I searched my pockets and discovered I had less than a credit left. I found the cheapest belt I could and begged the store owner to forgive me the rest of its price. Then I cinched it securely to the left and vowed to endure my poverty and hardship as a penance for my previous life."

He nattered on as they walked for another half mile. He took whatever job he could find, often sleeping in the streets because he gave his earnings to someone in even more desperate need than he was. There were a lot of jobs. A lot of dirty, boring jobs. Dirty boring jobs that somehow deserved to be extemporized in agonizing detail.

At least it was a straight corridor with hallways that branched out for residential quarters. How big had this station gotten? Dex wondered, then made himself make some inane comment to prove he'd been listening. It wasn't as hard as he'd thought; since the Elomijan repeated so much, he had a good chance of being on-topic even if his mind wandered. Still, Dex swore that if this story made him miss the directions to his apartment, he was going to use his new friend's belt as a gag.

"Then came the fateful day I was hired onto *Hudon's Revenge*. We were not bunked by rank, but availability. Though I was a lowly laborer, there to move crates and clean corridors, I had the good fortune of sharing quarters with the navigator and the cartographer." The navigator, Barajni, taught him about the Disk, and impressed by his aptitude, started letting him share the navigation duties.

"Of course, it was just an excuse to give him more time to indulge in his own hedonistic bad habits." Serani shrugged, and his tongue touched the right corner of his mouth.

Dex had seen Dolon do that when she was saying something ironic, too.

Finally, the story was getting somewhere.

Georj interrupted to point out a landmark to Dex, which apparently was culturally interesting but not navigationally significant. Then Georj drew the conversation back to Serani. "Being apprenticed to the navigator was a most fortunate turn of events for you, but did your captain not object? Adept as you claim to be, you were not schooled."

"The Captain didn't care, as long as the ship did what it was supposed to. That is how he thought of us, equipment and crew—The Ship. Just as Elomijans and Humans are The People. It seemed liberating at first, but I began to realize that it just excused him to use us as he did machinery."

The Captain, he said, was a cruel and greedy man, his crew an ever-changing roster of desperate people that came and went with about as much notice as replacement parts in the engines. When the navigator died by his own filthy habits, he was chucked out the airlock by his friends, and Serani took his place.

"But not his bunk—too many temptations found their way there. I was not ready for that kind of test."

Georj interrupted again to lead them into a less crowded corridor on the left, and Serani, declaring that this was his path as well, continued with his story. Dex feigned delight. Despite his physical therapy and walks with Dolon around the hospital, he was getting tired and his feet felt sore from the different flooring. A headache was forming behind his ears—one of the fun new sensations he'd had to get used to. He was ready for the comfort of a reclining chair in a quiet apartment.

Serani, oblivious to Dex's discomfort, backed up to review how he'd trained as a navigator while watching his mentor slowly kill himself. It had renewed his determination to stay clean. The crew was usually paid in drugs and prostitutes, he said, but the quartermaster respected Serani's choice and paid him in credits, and even helped him set up accounts at various stations.

"It was not much, of course. The Captain, as I said, was greedy, keeping most of the spoils for himself. He would account to the authorities as little of a run as he could get away with and shared with us as little of the profits as he could. I sometimes wonder what treasures he had found and never shared. At first, it didn't bother me, but as he began to expect more of my navigation skills, I knew talent would only take me so far. I needed more education. I started speaking with other navigators, and that, my friends, is when I realized how bad was the lot I'd chosen."

Four years ago, station time, Serani said, they'd returned from scavenging one of the greatest finds of the generation, but it had also been the most dangerous, and it had changed his mind as surely as when he'd fled the Pleasure Paths.

Something pinged in Dex's mind, pulling him more attentively to the conversation. Dolon had said the ship that found him had left about four years ago, station time, and returned almost immediately, shiptime, with him in a stasis field. Dex forgot his sore feet and boredom. "This find—was it near the event horizon?"

"The best finds are, as I'm sure you know. But yes, very close, and very perilous, especially since the Captain—I'd never learned his name, not in three years, subjective—insisted on keeping the ship hidden among the swarls and snatching at the stray pieces fate sent along our path."

The ship took a lot of damage, which Serani catalogued in great detail. Each hull crack and equipment failure tore at Dex with memories of his own fight for survival on the

Santiago. But not once in the long litany did he mention what they recovered. Just as Dex was about to stop in the hallway and shout for him to get to the point, Serani moved on.

"The Captain and I argued over the unnecessary risks. So, when we put in for repairs, I took my share of the profits, or rather what the quartermaster would give me, not knowing how valuable anything we recovered truly was. I am in a modest dwelling while I determine my next adventure."

Brenna now pointed to a nearly empty corridor on the right, this one lined with doors at even intervals. Again, Serani stayed with them. This time, Dex was glad he had.

"Near the event horizon?" Dex asked again, his heart hammering with hope. "I've heard of some impressive finds there lately. Was it scavenging the wreckage of the relic ship and one of the ancient People's?"

"The People of the Bloody Road, yes. Two of their ships, actually. There was a drone, as well."

He forced his voice to stay casual. "Did you ever find out exactly what you picked up?"

Serani shrugged. "I do not know. I had enough concentrating on keeping the ship hidden yet out of danger. They said I must be Elomij-kissed to have kept us alive."

"The *Hudon's Revenge* was lucky to have you, to be sure. When did you make port?"

"A week ago. I was gone seven months, subjective, but nearly four years, station time. I may be as new to the Keldar as you."

He bit back a mocking reply. In Dex's time, a four-year skip in time was a quick trip. Thanks to new technologies, though, ships moving through the accretion disk were able to mitigate some of the time dilation. Of course, the technology itself was centuries old and beyond Dex's understanding.

He stuck to the important issue. "It's been somewhat longer for me. Will your Captain have sold everything by now?"

Georj nudged him again, a warning that his abruptness was bordering on rude.

Serani, however, seemed to misunderstand Dex's intent. He patted Dex's arm with the back of his fingers. "Your concern is touching, my new friend, but unnecessary. The Captain never revealed the true value of our finds, so we learned to be content with what we received. We truly were the most desperate of crews, and most moved on as soon as they found a new opportunity. Still, worry not. The quartermaster was a fair man.

I have enough to care for my own needs and to help some of those in the hell levels of the Pleasure Paths who were good to me in my untamed youth."

Brenna pulled them to a stop before a teal-blue door with a braided frame. "This is it, Dex. Quarters, projective; home, conditional."

Home, if I want it to be. Do I want it to be? Dex felt his mouth go dry and forced himself not to sigh.

Serani, however, beamed. "You have done well for yourself, then-ship's captain."

Dex heard the question in the statement. "Dex. Call me Dex. And negative, definite. I wasn't especially successful. I was a small op— just me and my AI. Before that, my wife, some apprentices. We treated them as family. But my last mission was a desperate attempt to..."

His voice trailed off. What had driven him to go after that relic ship, when he could have—*should have*—snagged easier pray and pulled into Keldar for repairs? Why hadn't he released the Civ B ship at the first sign of trouble, instead of desperately hanging on and letting it drag him across the event horizon?

"It...was desperate," he concluded lamely.

Serani regarded him thoughtfully, then his face broke into a gentle grin. "Then we've much in common, friend. You seem to me a good man, Dex. Would that I had been part of your family." He removed his arm. "My own quarters are in a more modest section, so I shall take my leave and continue my journey. However, I would appreciate crossing paths in the future."

"Please, come soon. Anytime you are available. I've nothing pressing on my schedule and would like to know more about this fabulous and dangerous find. You know where I live."

Apparently, that was an idiom not in use in this era. Serani's eyes sparkled with amusement, and he held out his hands, wrists crossed, palms down. "And may your life be full of beauty and change. Yours as well, Georj."

They made their goodbyes, with Serani thrice more expressing his admiration of Dex and his joy at making new friends, and Dex also repeating his invitation, his chest growing tighter with impatience each time. He must have successfully kept that tension off his face because from behind Serani, Brenna nodded approvingly, then added his multiple expressions of regret that he was leaving soon and would not be able to continue their fine conversations until much later.

Finally, Dex and Georj crossed their wrists, palms up, and received Serani's farewell blessing.

When Serani had turned down a new corridor, Dex whirled to face Georj. "Can you find out about this *Hudon's Revenge?*"

"Let's get inside, first," his friend replied.

Georj pulled a chip from his pocket and slipped it into a slot. A panel by the door began to glow. He led Dex through procedures for the hand and retinal scan and the voice recognition, then removed the chip and handed it to him.

"Store this safely. You can use it to program others to enter your home. For temporary arrangements, you can instruct the AI to admit people under certain circumstances, as well."

Dex pressed his hand against the panel again, and the door opened to let them in.

"Good afternoon, Dex Hollister," the mellow, genderless voice of the house AI said. "Welcome and hospitality, projective and objective. You have one message from Dolon Scenza. She will pick you up at the sixth chime to make good on your wager."

Georj said, "Dolon keeps track of all the ships making port and their sales. She no doubt is aware of the *Revenge*. You can ask her tonight."

It was probably the straightest answer he'd ever gotten from the young historian, and yet, it answered nothing. Georj had nothing to contribute, apparently. Not even some asinine tangent. Or was he aware of Dex's weariness and was trying to humor his need for brevity?

Dex wandered his new place. The quarters were smaller than the living space aboard the *Santiago*, yet the open floor plan made them seem roomier. A counter separated the small kitchen from the living area. He peeked into the cabinets and found them lightly stocked with foods he recognized from the hospital.

"We thought it best to get you some familiar things until you can expand your tastes," Georj explained. "However, there is one thing I thought you'd enjoy."

He pulled out a bottle of amber liquid and two glasses. "It's a personal favorite of mine, from the vineyards of Kal Edani."

As he poured, Dex explored the two doors leading out of the living room. The bathroom had a shower stall—sonic—and a toilet that folded out of the wall. The bedroom, connected by a second adjoining door, was just large enough for a single-person sleeping mat and a chest for clothing and sundries. He found only a change of clothing and a few items Dolon had managed to buy back from the salvage: a piece of a column from the *Santiago's* kitchen area, with a daisy painted on it, an entertainment tape that miraculously survived... He wondered if he could get it re-recorded. Maybe he could re-introduce holos and make a fortune. Wouldn't that have made Scarlet laugh? He returned the recording to its place and took the piece of column to put in the kitchen. Daisies belonged in the kitchen.

He turned, then stopped cold, a gasp caught in his throat.

On the wall, the portrait of Scarlet and him from their honeymoon smiled back at him.

Where had that been hidden? When the Blacksone's had gotten to the point that the portrait had caused him to lose himself in memories, he'd ordered Santiago and Molly, his apprentice at the time, to get rid of it before he relived some memory that might get them both killed. He'd thought they had destroyed all the hard images, keeping the electronic files safely tucked in Santiago's memory banks. Had Molly tucked this one away somewhere in the hope they'd find a cure?

If so, Santiago had to have helped her. She knew every cranny on the ship; only he knew the ones Dex would never go into.

"You were a sentimental fool, Santiago," he muttered. He stepped to the painting as if approaching a shrine.

They had been so young, and she, so beautiful. Her hair rich and lustrous...

Georj cleared his throat from the doorway, but Dex didn't move until Georj had come in and set a glass in his hand. He, too, admired the woman in the painting.

"Beauty to rival Elomij," he said.

"You don't know the half of it." The words dredged themselves hoarsely from his dry throat. He sipped the drink, barely noticing the woody taste.

Georj set a hand on his shoulder, a human gesture that felt wrong to his skin and right to his heart. "If you need anything, the AI can contact me."

Dex nodded, and Georj let himself out. Dex was alone, truly alone for the first time since... Since before Scarlet.

He took the picture from the wall and sat on the bed, drinking and remembering how the light caught in the waves of Scarlet's beautiful hair.

CHAPTER FOUR

Scarlet sat on the beach towel with her arms around her bare legs. She bit her lip and tension made little wrinkles around her eyes, but Dex was too caught up with how the sun played with the highlights in her hair to notice.

"Doesn't it all make you nervous?" she asked.

He felt as far from "nervous" as a man could get, but he sat up, anyway. "All what?"

"All that water. The sand. All that...vastness."

She waved her hand to take in the sparsely populated beach. In the distance, some people were playing a game with a ball and net. To the other side, a mother and child searched for seashells, while in the water, while the father was helping another child swim. Toward the horizon, a couple of people rode the surf on narrow boards. Did the lack of people bother her, too? Probably. She'd lived on a station all her life.

He set his chin on her shoulder. "Space is vast, you know."

"True, but it's different. I mean, don't you get claustrophobic on Keldar?"

"Not really."

She shrugged him off so she could turn to face him. She had that "oh, really?" look that made him want to grin. He fought to keep his face straight, but he could feel in his cheeks that he was failing.

"You gripe about the crowds." she pointed out.

"Yeah, but that's people. Tight spaces don't bug me."

"Mmm-hmm. And it has never bothered you that the only thing between you and the vacuum of space is some shielding and metal plating?"

He shrugged. "Guess I'm adaptable."

Finally, she caught his not-quite-grinning grin. She smiled back. "All right. I can be adaptable, too. But I'm not sure I'm ready for that much water, yet."

"Okay. Today, let's dip our toes in. We have a lifetime of opportunities. I'll get you swimming eventually."

He stood and held out his hand. She took it and let him pull her into his arms, but broke free before he could embrace her fully. She ran to the beach, laughing, and he understood what she wanted.

When he caught up with her, he scooped her up over one shoulder and carried her, squealing protests between laughs, until they were waist-deep in the water. He dumped her in with mock carelessness, but slowly enough that she went feet first.

She shrieked with surprise at the cold water, hanging onto his neck. After a moment, her grip loosened, and she moved away, turning slowly, letting her hands drag around the waves. Her laughter became breathy, like a child caught between excitement and insecurity.

"See?" he said. "Not so bad once you make up your mind."

She stared out at the approaching waves, but this time, her expression was one of awe. "I love your courage, Dex," she said without turning around. "I love that you make me brave, too."

* * *

By the time the house AI announced that Dolon Scenza was requesting admittance, Dex had showered, changed, checked his belt, and was sitting in the recliner while the wall screen played news clips and public records on multiple screens. He'd not been allowed to view anything about his accident; the doctors wanted him to concentrate on his recovery. Now, he was determined to catch up and find some leads of his own.

He hollered for the computer to admit Dolon, then waved her to his chair. "Look at this," he said, expanding one of the screens to a record he'd been studying.

"*Hudon's Revenge*?" She draped an arm around the back of his chair with familiar ease. She wore a light scent, and despite his mission, it distracted him. He glanced her way. Her tunic had a high neck but open sides, with a wrap of fabric giving teasing glimpses of her pelt and skin beneath. Her belt was a simple thick ribbon tied in a loose knot. He wondered what it meant even as his hands itched to pull at the tie. He forced his gaze upwards and saw her short hair was decorated with beads and feathers that refracted the light into rainbow hues that played over her pale skin.

"You look amazing." The words had left his mouth before he knew he'd wanted to say them. A good thing, too. That funny combination of excitement and guilt rose again. Had he felt it before speaking, he would have kept his mouth shut. As it was, he felt the heat of embarrassment his internal conflict inspired. He knew it had to show on his face.

Even so, she gave him a grin, and he saw the dilation of her pupils; then, she returned her attention to the information on the screen. "Doing my job now? I did check the cargo manifest of *Hudon's Revenge*: mostly scrap metal, some burned out-engine parts..."

"Their captain doesn't claim all his finds. Is there such a thing as a black market in this age?"

She pulled back to face him fully. "And where did you hear this information?"

He shrugged but gave her a smug grin. "You walk the paths; you hear the gossip."

Her tongue flicked out, touching the corner of her mouth. His human mind thought how cute she looked doing that, and although his body didn't quite respond the way it might have in his past life, its reaction was decidedly pleasant.

"I have contacts in the Hidden Paths," she admitted, "though I try not to use them often. It can get...tricky. How certain are you of this information?"

He shrugged. "It seemed an innocent enough conversation. Navigator of the *Revenge*—former navigator—mentioned the mission while telling Brenna and me the story of his life. The. Whole. Story. That happen a lot here?"

"Perhaps we should stroll the paths so you may find out for yourself? I will make some inquiries into *Hudon's Revenge*. Tomorrow. But now, you must enjoy your victory in our little contest. That is our way."

He glanced back at the screen. Patience was so hard, but there was a beautiful woman standing before him, hand outstretched, offering to help make it easier.

Guess I need the practice.

She giggled, and he realized he'd spoken aloud.

"Practice in enjoying yourself? Is it such an alien concept, or were you truly that old?"

He heard the challenge in her light banter. "I'm a lot younger than I was," he said, and rising from the couch, he offered her his elbow.

"Please, elaborate!" she teased as she took it.

Suddenly, that felt too personal. He tensed.

She squeezed his arm, as if she'd sensed his anxiety and sympathized. "Perhaps that is a story for another time. I know you docked on this station often in your past life. Tell me: what did you do for fun, then?"

With a safer topic of conversation, they left his apartment.

They strolled arm-in-arm down the quiet corridor, Dex regaling her with a story of how, before he'd met Scarlet, he and his buddy had gone to a bar to pick up women, and he'd ended up in a fight instead. Dolon laughed and in the flowery and polite language of her people, called him an idiot.

"How was I supposed to know that was his girl?"

"I'd have thought her hitting you on the back of the head with a serving tray would be an indication."

"That was after I punched him back. Before that, she was only too eager to flirt with me. I'm sure I mentioned that thrice. Keep up," he teased.

"Ah, yes. Dex Hollister, the Irresistible...until the steady mate shows up."

"So, you were paying attention."

"Of course, I can see why no woman would resist your charms. Perhaps it would be best for you to avoid the Pleasure Paths. We would not want to disrupt the already hedonistic activities going on there."

"I'm not above a little hedonism, within reason. I would not knowingly take another man's mate. But I can hold my own in a fight. I got away with just a black eye that night."

"A black eye by the angry mechanic who came at you with a wrench he apparently had on his person just for smashing rivals," she repeated from his story, "plus a bump on the head from the platter?"

He snickered. "Yeah, that hurt for a day or two. Point being, I knew how to fight, duck, and run then, and I still do now. Probably know that better than how to have a conversation. Speaking of, what's with the corridors? We haven't seen anyone yet."

Despite the emptiness of the hallways, she was leaned in close. He was aware of every touch, and decided that despite circumstances, he liked it. He'd never thought he could feel like that again.

"This is typical of the dinner hour. Meals are for conversation as much as nutrition. Tonight is not a usual night for dining out, so the food carnival won't be as crowded as social days," she said. "This is good, though. I think it would have been overwhelming."

He thought about his first day on the beach with Scarlet. "I'm not one for just sticking my toes in." Uninvited, he launched into retelling her the memory he'd been thinking about only hours before. When he finished, he was as surprised as she was.

She unlinked her arm from his and stood in front of him, blocking his way. She held her hands in front of her, fingers up. "Thank you. I think that was the most meaningful story you've ever shared with me. You showed me a glimpse of the path you walked, and it makes the path we travel a bit clearer."

He touched his fingertips to hers, acknowledging her gratitude. Then he crooked his elbow to her. "I think that's probably my version of 'waist deep.' Don't expect too much more from me today."

She chuckled and resumed her place as his walking companion. "As you once said, we have many opportunities. Let us speak of present things. Do your quarters suit you?"

"Very nice—and thank you, for the things you found, especially the picture and the bit of painted wall."

"I have a list of other items that you may wish to reclaim for sentimental reasons. We can go over later. Those seemed the most personal, and I wanted you to have something to welcome you."

"They did." His throat had gone dry, and he turned his attention to the abstract designs on the walls.

It was just lines in a riot of colors. They started together at one end of the corridor, a little wobbly but moving in unison; then they split and filled the wall: swirling, jerking, doubling back... Where they crossed, they formed shapes according to the number of lines at the intersection—triangles, squares, even a reasonably symmetric dodecahedron.

"Each year, the secondary schools are given a corridor for a project. It's always interesting to see how tastes change over the years." Dolon said. She segued into a story of her class's project, and Dex grunted, his focus on the wall. The first impression was chaos, but if he concentrated, he could follow one line. He stepped back, his mind insisting there had to be a pattern in the hole. Dolon kept pace obligingly. She said something about seeing things through new eyes. He squinted, and the lines seemed to move, to form a face.

The Goddess Elomij winked at him.

"Life is change. Does she look the same—your wife?"

"What?" His gaze jerked from vision to Dolon's face. Her eyes were wide, and her mouth set in an attitude of curiosity.

"Wife, projective, past. I seek no story. I am merely curious: When you look at Scarlet's picture with Elomijan-Human eyes, does she look the same?"

"I...hadn't thought about it." He glanced back at the wall, but it had returned to a chaos of lines. They strolled in silence as he pondered her question, until they entered a busier area. Another couple, heading in the opposite direction, stopped in front of them and initiated a conversation.

They introduced themselves as Nira and Nolan Tasus, shopkeepers. Nira admired Dex's outfit while Nolan and Dolon talked about what they bought and sold. As they spoke, the corridor started to fill with people, heading to the food carnival or returning home, carrying cartons of take-out. The smells made the hall seem even more crowded and started Dex's stomach rumbling. He held back an impatient sigh as Nira completed a story about designing a tunic for her cousin.

Then, Nira announced they were expecting their first child at the end of the year. As Dolon and he gave their congratulations, Dex said a silent thanks that they did not launch into the story of the child's conception.

"But you've not spoken much!" Nolan said to him.

"Guess I've not much to say," he replied, "and I must admit my stomach is doing much speaking to me."

Nira and Nolan laughed as if that were a great joke. "You sound almost human when you say that," Nolan confided, but they let it go, thanked them for an interesting conversation, and moved on.

Dex watched their retreating backs.

"They couldn't tell I was human." For some reason, the thought made him shiver.

Dolon leaned into his arm. "They didn't look closely enough. Your bone structure is too broad, and your fingernails too thick. And of course, you retain your human reticence for speaking."

"Plenty of gabby humans," he responded automatically. He looked at his hands, the wide palms the short, thick nails. Three fingers. Was there so little of his humanness left?

"This bothers you?"

"Yes and no. I'm grateful. I truly am. But then, there are moments... I've lost so much—now, my humanity, too?"

She chucked his chin with the back of her hand. "You have your mind. The sum of your intellect and experiences. Your past, your present, and your future. You still have the same soul that has always been Dex Hollister. Even among the Elomijans, some things do not change. Do not forget that you are Dex Hollister, and you will always retain the best of your humanity."

He stared into her serious, earnest eyes and digested her words. Around them people, Elomijan and Human, flowed, but no one stopped. It was if they knew the importance of that moment for Dex and Dolon and respected their privacy.

"You're right." He took a deep breath, held it, and released it slowly. "I'm still Dex Hollister, no matter how else I change."

"Change is beauty," she caressed his jaw with the back of her fingers, and he shivered at the sensation.

His stomach growled, breaking the spell, and they laughed as they headed at a quicker pace to the food district.

The dining plaza was blocked by a gate with an automated teller. Dolon placed her hand over the sensor plate, spoke her name and said, "Feasts for two." They placed their hands into an opening which stamped them, and they were admitted.

She led him in a couple of steps, then pulled him aside so he could take in the plaza without blocking the way of other diners.

It really was a carnival, or maybe a cacophony. Booths and shops popped up at random in the large plaza. Food booths snugged against art studios and clothing stores as if greasy fingers were welcome. He spotted at least three stages that rotated talent: dancers, storytellers, and artists creating works as people watched.

People crowded the aisles, such as they were; only now, instead of stopping to talk, they were also sticking food into each other's mouths. He felt almost as much as heard the noise: song, laughter, the never-ending conversations...

He swallowed hard. He'd told Scarlet he never got claustrophobic, and he never had. Until now.

Again, Dolon squeezed his arm reassuringly. He focused on her and the feeling passed as quickly as it had come.

"We shall go in waist-deep," Dolon said. "There is too much to see in a single evening, or even a full day, anyway. Once you've been here a few times, you'll get used to it."

Dex snorted. "You forget. I am Dex Hollister, relic hunter, Captain of the *Santiago*. No one could navigate the swarls like me. This is just an accretion disk made of people."

Dolon smiled. Dex couldn't tell if she was impressed or amused, but it didn't matter. She was cute when her nose wrinkled like it had. She said, "Then I shall be your navigator. Course, Captain?"

The smells, too, were boisterous and rich, but some were familiar enough. "Food!"

They stepped into the fray. As they walked, Dolon explained. "The stamps are sensitive to caloric intake. I bought us the maximum. We can wander about and try anything you like and stay until you are ready to go home. But you must promise to try to talk. Human though you are, bad conversation means bad digestion."

"Is that true? Is that why they fed me that pabulum at the hospital?"

Dolon laughed a merry staccato. "It's simply an old saying. My mother would chide me often: 'Bad conversation means bad digestion.' Perhaps I have a bit of human in me, too."

"Are you part human, then?" an older human in shirt and trousers interrupted to address Dex. "Thought you might be."

"Yes. I...needed a DNA splice. Saved my life. Dex Hollister." He started to hold out his hand, remembered that palm-to-palm contact was considered intimate among the Elomijans, and pulled back in embarrassment.

The elderly man grasped him by the wrist. "Lucky for you, then, Dex. Arbon Grays. I work in station environmental systems, air scrubbing. Interesting job, air scrubbing. People don't often appreciate how much work it takes to keep all the smells and pollutants at bay."

Dex's chest ached with the memory of his lungs burning from the acrid air in the *Santiago* after they'd been dragged across the event horizon the first time. "I captained an independent trading ship. Did the job myself, and I know what it's like when those systems fail. I very much appreciate your work. I would think a place like this keeps you busy."

"Indeed!" he said and regaled them with a story about an unlucky fire in the haspla booth had led to a gritty week of hand washing all the filters in the section. "We didn't have enough nanites. Haspla makes an especially slimy, smelly smoke," he concluded, then led them in a discussion about the worse smoke smells. With all the damaged systems on the *Santiago* during their last adventure, Dex found he had a few opinions to share.

So, for the next few hours, they talked and ate, the conversations as varied as the food, and not all to Dex's liking. Through example, however, Dolon taught him the right questions to ask, the polite way to move on, even when it was and was not appropriate to speak with one's mouth full. They worked up their own secret signals. Dolon settled on the kick to the ankle when he committed some faux pas. It seemed some signals were universal, after all.

Meanwhile, if he snuck his arm around her waist and drummed his fingers on her hip, she knew they needed to move on, lest he resort to "uh-huh" or burst out with an impatient "The short of it!" It wasn't always impatience that drove him to move on, of course. It was one thing to come to terms with being a man 600 years out of his time; quite another to broadcast it to the world. Even without people thinking he was the Huntradex—and it relieved him that no one even thought of it—he was not ready to share the details of his past with strangers who had not earned the right to invade his privacy. Another attitude he would have to adjust.

Even more, some conversations were just hard. He'd grown accustomed to the syntax of the People and picked up some of the slang thanks to the adventures Cej had loaned him. But he missed jokes, only laughing because Dolon was, and tried not to show confusion when they talked about technology these people took for granted. He wasn't sure he could do Arbon Gray's job, much less captain a ship again, and it gave him a sick feeling in his stomach.

"I have to go back to school," he told Dolon as they shared a plate filled with finger foods; one of each, so that they shared bites. At first, it had felt too intimate for this crowded venue, never mind that everyone around them was doing the same thing. This particular booth specialized in new culinary experiences. Thus, it was expected that everyone nibble, share, and not enjoy everything on their plate but still savor the experience and variety.

He set down a green ball of something whose bitterness made him wince. "Problem is, I don't even know where to start. Georj told me he learned about the respirating trees in grade school. How far back will I have to go?"

Dolon picked up the tidbit he'd abandoned and popped it into her mouth.

"Perhaps you could set up a dawlsu booth? But worry not. There are classes specific for relic hunters out of their time, and special tutors. I'll get you some names once you are more settled. For now, relax, get to know this new world. You do not have to do everything at once. After all, even children learn social skills before being taught about respirating trees."

"So, I'm a child, now?"

She shrugged lightly, then they both started laughing. A 698-year-old child.

After that, Dolon steered conversations away from occupations and technology and to softer pursuits. They stopped at a stage and watched an artist create incredible designs by dipping her fingers into different colors of paints and swirling them in time to music played by her partner on a kind of multiple pipes. The woman was graceful enough, but Dex fought to not roll his eyes every time her fingers brushed the canvas, and someone applauded.

One of the most enthusiastic clappers stood beside him. "Isn't she wonderful?" the man asked, though he clearly expected unquestioning agreement. "That's Alice her-Ashto. She's one of the top talents in this sector. Her work is in planetary capital buildings, museums, and the homes of the wealthiest families. Yet whenever she's in port, she hires a local musician, finds a stage, pays her performance fee, and sells her creations like any other artist. I've followed her career since I was a boy. She is truly gods-kissed, and yet stays so humble."

He stopped then to clap and cheer as she did a pirouette and splattered some green onto the canvas.

By the end of the song, Dex was impressed enough to agree to look at the works she had displayed at a small booth. He purchased one for Dolon and one for himself.

"It looks like a rainstorm in this meadow near where I grew up," he said as he held it out at arms' length. At the urgings of those around him, he launched into a long description of the flowers, the rain, his younger sister spinning and dancing, a chain of flowers in each hand.

He enjoyed the evening far more than he'd expected.

"I thought you would," Dolon said when, in the privacy of his quarters, he told her that. "Once you relaxed and realized people would not treat you as a curiosity or a legend, but simply as one of the People."

"You were the one wanting to walk arm in arm with a six-century-old relic," he teased as he pressed the painting against a wall where he could see it from the kitchen. He stepped back to admire it, and Dolon moved close behind him, her hands on his shoulders.

"I think you know I meant more than that, don't you, my Huntradex?"

He took in a sharp breath.

She walked around so that she faced him. "Dex, I'm teasing."

"I know." He licked his lips. "It's just... In the Disk, and on the other side of the event horizon, I... I had visions. I thought it was because I'd been listening to the Elomijan legends, or maybe the Blacksone's was messing with my mind. They felt very real. Then this evening, the painting in the corridor. I swear, I saw her face."

Her head tilted. "You walked the Bloody Road?"

"Did I?" He shook his head. "Nothing's sure anymore. But in my hallucination or vision or whatever, Elomij made it pretty clear. To be Huntradex meant to belong to her."

"You turned down a goddess?"

"I guess I did." He raised a brow, tilted his head—and felt the tip of his tongue touch the edge of his lip.

She mimicked the expression. Then, she placed one hand on his chest and walked around him, letting her fingers trail across chest, arms, back. It sent shivers up and down his body that were at once alien and achingly familiar. "Well, if nothing is sure, how can you be sure I'm not Elomij, taking mortal form to woo the only one ever to deny me?"

She returned to her original position before him and smiled, her eyes sparkling with mischief. She held her hands to her sides, palms facing him in open invitation.

And he wanted to. Oh, how he wanted to. But her eyes...

He closed his own, blocking the sight of her. "I can't. I'm sorry. It's too soon. I need time."

"We have time, Dex Hollister. You are a find worth pursuing, and a most pleasant and beautiful change to my life. Tomorrow, I will seek out the *Hudon's Revenge* among my contacts and speak to you in the afternoon." Her fingertips brushed his lips, sending a shock through his system. He breathed in deeply by sheer reflex but did not move. Nor did he move or open his eyes as he heard her walk away. He didn't trust himself, but whether he would sweep her into his arms, or fall to his knees grieving, he didn't know.

He felt it: the vastness of an entire ocean, the beach, the horizon. The world reaching out and inviting him to dive in. It did make him nervous—and excited.

But he wasn't ready to do more than dip his toes.

Chapter Five

"Now you understand why I wear my buckle to the left," Georj said as they ate lunch in Dex's quarters the next day. He'd dropped by to bid Dex a quick farewell before heading to the docks for a transport back to his home, when he noticed the new painting and asked about it. Dex had surprised them both by giving him a full account of his date.

Dex hadn't intended to talk about it, especially about those last few minutes with Dolon. Was it because he was already adapting to Elomijan openness, or did he need to bounce his thoughts off someone else, someone who understood what he was going through? It had definitely been a date, and he'd spent a restless night going over the details in his mind.

Perhaps celibacy would be a good option. At least it'd be one less thing to adapt to.

Did it matter? He'd already committed to a packet—might as well commit to the entire hold. Why deny himself what might be the best part of his situation? "I don't know if can do that. I mean, I had, when Scarlet died. I never wanted another woman. But I was older. I had other things to keep me whole. Now... I'm not sure I want to. Maybe if I were in my original body—or even an older version of this one. Or maybe..."

"...if Dolon didn't suit you so well?" Georj raised a brow, and Dex couldn't help grinning. Outside the hospital setting, the historian had relaxed markedly, and Dex found himself enjoying his company all the more. He was going to miss his friend.

Must be the new body, he thought. Never much cared for company before.

Georj's expression turned serious. "Grief is a difficult thing, and because of your former condition, it seems to me you could not grieve in the normal way. Tell me more about Blacksone's. I read up on the medical literature, at the layman's level, of course. I understand that repeated exposure to the temporal tides of the Disk reworked neural pathways, sometimes, even made neurons 'skip,' but that's about all."

Dex shrugged and leaned back in his seat, rolling a glass between his thumb and finger. "You know about as much as I, then. I was one of the first to contract it; Santiago's shielding let us get deeper into the Disk than most. It's more than remembering. It's emphatically real. I would lose all track of time, sometimes even all sense of the world around me. I moved and spoke as if I were in whatever memory I was experiencing—but it wasn't a reenactment of the past. It felt as if I were in that time. It was very immediate."

He pointed to the artwork on his wall. "Now my past is more like that painting—indistinct and elusive. Yesterday, I stared at the portrait in my room for hours trying to remember Scarlet, trying to will myself into an experience of Scarlet. And I couldn't. There were impressions and snatches of memories, but disparate and vague." His hand clenched around his glass against the urge to throw it at the wall.

Georj nodded. "I remember the first time I couldn't recall Salia's smile. I skipped classes that day and just sat in the dark, hooked up to the VR, going over the recordings of our wedding and celebrations with friends. But it was like it was someone else's life."

"I made Molly destroy all my recordings when the Blacksone's started getting bad. Maybe it's just as well." Dex gave a sighing laugh. "Scarlet died over twenty years ago, subjective. You'd think I'd be over it by now."

Georj reached out and grasped his arm. "Dex, with everything that's happened, how can you not expect to grieve anew?"

Dex nodded. Just another thing he'd need to be patient about. He hoped Dolon could be patient, too.

* * *

Dolon returned in the afternoon, as promised, though wearing more modest clothing and a businesslike mien. That suited Dex just fine.

Settling into the chair beside his, she faced the screen and fed some information into his computer. An image appeared of a large, bulbous ship, whose patchworked and scored hull could have made a darker rival to some of the abstracts lining the corridors.

"Behold, the *Hudon's Revenge*." She accepted the drink he handed her—a light fruity punch she'd introduced him to last night.

He sat on the edge of his chair, elbows on knees, his own tumbler of juice in his hands. "Ugly ship."

"With an even uglier crew. After the stories I heard this morning, I must doubt your taste in new friends."

"Serani isn't my friend. But, like I said, he seemed okay. Naïve, maybe. Kind of reminded me of an apprentice I picked up on the docks. Molly. She could have been hired on by some disreputable ship if it hadn't been for Scarlet. Turned out to be the best apprentice we ever had. Laser sharp, she was—and driven. Always pestering me for something more to do or learn... But a story for another time. What else did you learn?"

But she sighed and looked at him with sad eyes. "So, is this where we are again? I thought after last night..."

"What?" he asked a little more loudly than he intended. A little more panicked than he'd expected. What had happened last night? What social convention had he missed had he missed this time?

"You did well on your first night with the People yesterday, but you still don't understand. Conversation and the sharing of our stories is the great pleasure and most valued asset of the Elomijans. You gave me a small gift just now with the mention of Molly. But then you turned it into a tease. You would not waste my time by giving me a fuller accounting, and the promise of 'another time,' cheapens the value of the time we are sharing now."

"I thought you came here on business. I thought you had news about the *Revenge*. About Santiago."

"I see. The sharing is wasting your time, then?"

He'd been married long enough to know when he was treading on dangerous ground. She may have phrased it in generalities, but he had heard the unspoken accusation: *You think you're wasting time by socializing with me.*

"No, Dolon. That's not it. Not really, but... Well." He mashed his lips together, thinking hard for an analogy that might explain without insulting her. "It's like a cargo on a ship. Each thing has its assigned place. I'm glad to tell you about Molly, but another time. Right now, we're doing business."

She shook her head. "Remember the *brista Elomij* I introduced you to? They call it the social cake of my people."

"I remember," he said, settling himself down for a lesson. She'd told him this four times over the course of the evening. "But it's more than a dessert. It's a rite of passage. No Elomijan can reach majority without knowing how to bake one."

She nodded. "And the preparation takes hours. Some of the fruits must be soaked in a sweetener, others in a salt. Then, they are blended. When I was three, I decided I would make myself *brista*. Only, I didn't know how, of course. Instead, I sparked on the brilliant idea of lining up the ingredients and simply eating them one after another in succession. The berries were fine. The flour, bland and gritty. But I took one bite of the kishta root and got completely and violently sick. You can't eat kishta without soaking it in ella juice."

He rubbed his skull behind his ears against the headache he felt coming on. "Are you saying if we only talk business, you'll vomit?"

"I'm saying the Elomijans do not compart-mentalize. Not our food, not our cargo, not our business. This is how we have been from long before Unification. The pace of our soci-ety is defined by it."

"How do you get anything done? I mean, what about emergencies? Do you know how many times fast action and short sentences saved my skin? I'd have died a long time ago if every cry for help had to involve some long-winded discussion about how I once fell down a cliff."

"And when those situations call for it, we are just as taciturn as any human!" Dolon snapped. "If we weren't, you wouldn't be alive now. And as for getting things done, the Elomijans found you humans. *We* initiated relations. *We* developed the respirating trees and many of the technologies that have made it safer to travel in the Disk. And yet, *we* also find time to build deep friendships and to treasure the individuals we encountered.

"When I first visited you, the information I had would have taken minutes to report, but I planned for hours. And you cannot tell me you did not benefit from my presence. To be one of the People is to explore every aspect of the path you are on. We do not limit ourselves. It's an attitude you will need to learn."

What about relationships? He squashed the thought. That was a tangent he was not ready for. "You're right. I'll work on it. But for now—the *Revenge*?"

She blinked at him, clearly waiting for something, but he had no idea what. He'd asked her a question. What was she expecting? "Well?"

"It cannot always be 'a story for another time.' We are here. We are alone. Molly was important enough to bring up. Tell me more."

"What's there to tell? She's dead and has been 500 years. Can we concentrate on the issue at hand—Santiago, who may still be out there and rescuable?"

She sighed. "You heard what I said, yet your feet stay stuck to your path. Will finding Santiago help you move on or cement you more firmly in your place?"

The thought stung. "Can we please cross that void when we get to it?

Her expression grew hard, and she turned back to the screen. She made her report in tense, clipped tones. "You saw the manifests of items they claimed; I've uploaded those that have been sold, along with images where available. Yours was not the only salvage the *Revenge* sold when in port at that time. The ship remained at Keldar for two weeks for repair, crew R&R—mostly in the Pleasure Paths, I'm told—and to pick up a new navigator, so Serani's story checks out there, at least. The captain, Glish Unistas, logged a claim to a sector near your re-emergence from the black hole for the next six months, objective, was denied, and logged a second request closer to the event horizon. They left port eleven weeks ago and have not been heard from in five."

"So, we'll have to wait them out?"

Dolon shook her head. "The ship was outfitted with an automatic locator beacon—unreported to captain or crew and hidden from the ship's AI. Port Authority had begun to suspect that the *Hudon's Revenge* was not sticking to its flight plans nor reporting all its prizes to customs. They lost signal four weeks, three days ago. Ship and crew have been logged as missing presumed destroyed, and since you will ask: no, no one will launch rescue or go after them seeking salvage. The ship was neither well-loved nor particularly valuable."

Dex took a long swallow of his drink. *This can't be a dead end. It just can't.*

"My contact at Port Authority couldn't give me complete details, but he could tell me that Unistas' deposits exceeded the amount he claimed in sales. I've also learned that he made some rather hefty purchases in illegal substances and higher-quality courtesans than usual."

"Serani said that's how he paid the crew. Sounds like they got a bonus."

"Sounds like they discovered something of significant value. I have some feelers out, but we are dealing with an unscrupulous element."

He cocked his head. "Could it be dangerous?"

She shrugged, as if she took that as par for the course. "It could be expensive."

"Do it—everything I have is at your disposal."

She frowned and sat up to turn in her chair to face him. "Dex, are you certain about this?"

What kind of stupid question was that? "Santiago and I had 70 years together. He saved my hide more times than I can count. If I run low on funds, I'll get a job. Do you find those for people as well?"

She nodded calmly, but he saw the tension in her neck and jaw. "Should this path lead you to such a need, I can ask around. In the meantime, let us double-check the items Unistas did claim for any clues."

She pulled up another file, this one with photos and descriptions. She led him through them one by one, her voice professional, her words curt even by his standards. Her gaze remained fixed on the screen, her jaw set, all personal sharing and even lectures on social graces locked into their own compartments.

What's bothering her? he wondered when she flipped to another slide without comment. This is more than me being a jerk. Is she afraid she'll fail?

"Look," he said as gently as he could, "I know that you can't guarantee that you'll find him..."

She cut him off. "I will make every effort and if it can be done, I will do it before you spend yourself broke. Now what is this 'rubber cuff seal'?"

He sighed, more of a growl. If she wanted to be like that, then, fine. "It's part of the toilet. Worthless. Next?"

An hour later, Dolon's mood had calmed, but his had gotten worse. They were no closer to a lead than when they'd started.

Dex howled at the next image that showed up, a tangle of lines labeled "wires and plating." He lurched out of the chair and began to pace. "'Wires!' 'Plating!' What kind of plating? Hull or interior? Qaduranium or simple steel?"

"It's a trick hunters use," Dolon said. "They keep purposely vague so they can adjust the claim."

"I know it's a trick!" he yelled. "The trick is over six hundred years old. *Six hundred years*, and Port Authority *still* hasn't found a way to stop people from using that *trick*?" He grabbed his head, fingers digging into his hair, heels of his hands pressing into his eyes.

Dolon went to him and placed her hands on his shoulders, fingers finding the pressure points and rubbing in small circles. "Perhaps we should leave this for a time? Go get some dinner. There is an interesting lecture series on the mammalian flying species of Oridian Six. You like animals, correct?"

"Don't patronize me!" He pulled away from her. "Warblers, really? You think I want to waste my time listening to people talk about creatures my father taught me about as a child, when the last friend I have could still be lost out there?"

Dolon blinked; then she crossed her arms. "Understand, projective, imperative, Dex Hollister. Your chances of finding your ship's AI intact and in any condition to be transferred to a new system is about par with the chances you had of surviving two trips through the event horizon."

"Well, we did that, didn't we?"

"Yes. *You* did. You are one of the most gods-touched beings I've ever known. And I believe in the gods-touch, or I would not be wasting my time with you and this ridiculous search!"

"I'm paying you," he snarled.

She tossed her head, making the jeweled feathers in her hair flip. "You think my profit is that great? I could be making twice what I am with half the effort!"

"Then why are you bothering?"

"Because you fascinate me, Dex Hollister. First your case, and then you. And because you need someone. You even said it yourself: we did that. You *and* your computerized friend. And now you are in a world even more alien than the one you survived. You need a guide—and you need friends. And as *your friend,* I do not want to see you throw away all your earnings and any chance you have of making a new life for yourself with it, all in the reckless pursuit of a piece of your past!"

Scarlet would have poked him in the chest by now, and then stormed out of the room to let him mull over her words. Dolon, however, stood with crossed arms and stared him down.

In another life, Dex would have stormed out of the room himself, and spent some time brooding. But here, in this new life, he found his feet rooted to the floor and his gaze pinned by hers. After a long silence, Dex lowered his eyes and heaved a cleansing sigh. "Okay, you've made your point. But you need to understand this: My former life was all about risk. It's who I am, at the very core of my being, and a new body and a new world will not take that out of me. And if I am gods-touched, that is how. And if that means risking everything to find Santiago and failing, then I will do what I have always done: improvise, survive, and overcome."

"I know this about you," she said quietly.

"Do you? You invited me to hear a lecture on warblers. I grew up on the wildlife pre-serves where warblers roamed. My father was gamekeeper, and I worked at his side. Once, scaling a mountain, I slipped and fell forty feet onto an outcropping and broke my leg. In warbler territory. I could have waited for my father to rescue me. Instead, I grabbed a pass-ing warbler by the leg and let her carry me to the top of the cliff."

"It sounds terrifying," she said, but there was a sparkle in her eyes as she spoke.

He took her hand. "It was, but you have to understand: I didn't even think twice about doing it. I make my own fortune and forge my own paths."

Dex took a breath and then continued. "But you are right. I do need help here. I need friends. I want you to be my friend and my guide. But I don't want to go out to dinner, and I don't want to argue about Elomijan manners or the impossibility of finding my AI, and I don't want to go out socializing. I just want to continue searching that manifest."

She stared at him wide eyed, head cocked, and top lip curled back. It took a moment for him to recognize the look: surprise and sentiment. Brenna had worn it when Dex had opened up to him about Dolon. He realized he'd just diffused their argument by telling her a story. One he'd even alluded to earlier.

Then she cleared her throat and the moment was gone. "I would never wish to change the core of you, Dex Hollister. Never among the People have I known anyone with such determination. We shall look at manifests all night if need be. But you will eat. Even more than Humans, the Elomijan metabolism requires a steady caloric intake or mental acuity suffers."

"And perhaps mental stability?" He gave her his best self-depreciating grin.

Her eyelids shut and opened slowly. "That may be a character trait. But for now, let's adjourn to the kitchen. For one hour. I shall teach you to cook a simple meal, and we shall eat, and I will not lecture you but you may practice your listening skills while I share with you my stories—request imperative."

"One hour? Sounds like you're compartmentalizing."

"And you know that change is an Elomijan way. We can adapt. But do not push me, Dex Hollister."

Her fierce expression was only half in jest, but he couldn't help thinking how incredibly beautiful she was. "I'll try to remember. And I may be persuaded to spend a little more than an hour."

"Then let us step upon this path together and see where it leads." She crooked her elbow, and he slid his arm through hers.

They cooked and ate, and she told him stories of some of her more lucrative assignments, as well as some of the more ridiculous ones. He listened, laughed, and started to share his own stories—and the evening passed without notice until she declared that she needed to go home and sleep in order to make her morning appointments. They never got back to the manifest, but she left it for him to continue to look over in the morning.

Before she left, he brushed her cheek with the back of his fingers. "You fascinate me, too, Dolon Scenza."

CHAPTER SIX

"Dex Hollister!"

Dex excused himself from the conversation he was having and made his way across the tram car to where Serani stood waving by the door. He pointed to two empty seats, and they joined up there.

Serani crossed his wrists, fingers flexed and back of his palms toward Dex. Dex returned the greeting even as Serani started talking, "My new friend. It has been weeks since we saw each other. Where have your travels taken you today?"

"The docks," Dex replied. "Meeting with some new friends." Being in a good mood, he went into detail about lunch with Captain El-sani, a client of Dolon's, who had just come back from a disappointing run to discover that one of his previous finds had made him a fortune. They had been celebrating.

Of all the relic hunters Dolon had introduced Dex to, Elsani was one Dex got along best with, but he enjoyed hanging out around the docks. He was more comfortable there, especially around the Elders, some of whom were as young as Dolon, subjectively, but because of their adventures in the Disk, had lived through more than a century of station history. They understood his taciturn ways, even if they teased him it was bad manners stationside.

Besides, even after 600 years, these were his people: obsessed with the Disk and its mysteries, addicted to the rush of navigating its dangers, and always thinking about the next "catch." He'd spent many happy hours in competition over who had had the greatest find.

"Such a stroke of luck for your friend!" Serani said enthusiastically. "Does that mean he will retire now? Perhaps you will take on his ship?"

Dex sighed. Elsani had in fact suggested that. After all, his ship was only 300 years ahead of Dex's time. And a new challenge had presented itself: the emergence of a new swarl not far from where Dex had been discovered.

Elsani had spoken coaxingly. "You were one of the first to study swarls, and physics is eternal. Besides, we still know so little about what could have caused a new one after so many centuries. This is uncharted ground that you are skilled to explore."

Still, Dex had stalled. A couple of hunters had offered to take him on a run as their guest; an "orientation," they called it. Something stopped him from saying, "yes" to them, too.

Some of his friends would look from him to Dolon, who often sat beside him, shoulder to shoulder, and smile knowingly. The last time, one of their friends did not stop at a knowing grin.

"Let us not tempt Dex further," he said, "for what adventure can compare to that of courting someone so lovely and interesting as Dolon Scenza?"

The others raised their glasses in toast, but she turned toward Dex and spoke seriously. "I would not hold you back, Dex. You are a wonderful companion on the walk of my life, but if other greener paths await you elsewhere..." Her voice faded then, and he realized with a shock how much he meant to her, and how much she'd come to mean to him.

Still, that had not been why he hesitated.

"I need more time," Dex told Serani as he had told his friends. "The *Santiago* was my ship for over seventy years. The AI and I were a team. Extensions of each other. It's difficult to go back to that life when..." he shrugged. "It's just difficult."

Rather than tease him for his brief answer, Serani nodded seriously. The tram stopped, and when Dex made to leave, Serani looped his arm through Dex's and joined him. For a wonder, they walked in companionable silence, save for greeting those on the way.

When they got closer to Dex's home, Serani spoke, his tone serious and direct. "I may understand your feelings in my own way, Dex. I have been to the docks myself, speaking to captains, checking out ships, and yet I cannot make myself take that next step. It is not that I miss the *Hudon's Revenge*, of course!"

Dex barked out a laugh. "I'd hope not! As a captain, Unistas wasn't worth the thrust of a barge. That was your captain's name, by the way—Unistas. Though I understand why you never learned it." He relayed the story he'd heard from a former second mate of the Hudon's *Revenge*, about a crewman who had spoken Unistas' name in a way the captain thought sounded disrespectful and was subsequently shot out the airlock. After that everyone was instructed to call him only "Captain," and even then, with respect and a hint of awe. Even as he spoke, he wondered at how he was doing almost all the talking. Such a different experience from two weeks ago!

Serani nodded, "He was a terrible captain, indeed, and was never satisfied with anything less than slavish devotion. Which is, indeed, what baffles me: I have experienced the worst of ships: dangerous missions, hostile crewmates, little reward...."

"Are you a drennal? Sorry—old word. Someone who enjoys the rush of danger, who thrives on it. The best and the worst hunters are drennals. We take the crazy risks and go after the big rewards."

"Are you a 'drennal,'"? Serani asked.

They'd approached Dex's house. Without thinking, he palmed the door and invited Serani in. Only after he'd poured him a drink did he realize what he'd done. Dolon would be proud.

"I was. I was the best hunter of my generation, Serani. I was always after the next find, the more challenging, the better, and it took a lot to challenge my ship and me."

"And now?"

Dex felt a tightness in his chest. The last "challenge" destroyed Santiago. Had it destroyed the old Dex, not just the body, but the soul?

"I don't know. It was another lifetime."

Serani gripped his arm. "Yours is a unique case, but Elomij gifts her people with many lifetimes. I embraced a new life when I turned my back on the Pleasure Paths and their false promises of joy. It was not always easy. Even though my former life's path was full of rot and pain with little real to show for it, I would sometimes yearn for it. How much harder it must be for you, whose path was green and fruitful."

Why did he feel that, of all the people he'd met, Serani would most understand his plight?

Even so, he didn't know what to say next. What was there to say?

He changed the subject instead. "If you're not a drennal, why go back to the docks looking for work?"

Serani stammered a few minutes, then started a story about a fellow navigator he met and what they talked about. Just nattering, the kind of purposeless chatter that got under Dex's pelt. Dex looked past him, into the living room and the painting he'd bought because it reminded him of his sister dancing in a rainy meadow. As Serani heaped on detail after useless detail to his story, the details of the painting seemed to shift and move—and then Elomij was among the flowers, arms out-stretched languidly, face tilted to the clouds.

Then she looked down toward the two of them and yawned.

"Stop it!" Dex snapped.

"...and by coincidence, he... What?" Serani blinked, his narrative derailed.

Dex suppressed a groan. The last thing he wanted was for anyone to know he was hav-ing visions of their goddess. His mind floundered before latching onto his old impa-tience. "You have been talking nonstop for five minutes, yet nothing you've said ad-dresses my question. Elomijans may call that 'conversation' and 'sharing,' but in my time, we called it 'avoidance' and 'deflection,' and it's annoying as Corsha's void. Let me ask you something direct: When you dragged yourself out of the Pleasure Paths and that life, did you spend hours talking about it first?"

"We would often talk about how much we wanted a better life. I remember once—"

Dex held up a hand. "And when did you do something about it?"

Serani paused, his face a mix of surprise and guilt.

Dex smirked. "When you stopped talking."

* * *

"Serani Guln continues to request entrance," the AI reported with the same banal calm it had when it reported the Elomijan's presence the first three times.

Dex groaned. Even at half volume, the computerized voice made the pounding of his head flare like angry drumbeats. He'd already fielded three calls – one from Dolon, one from each of the friends they'd met with last night – and told them he just wanted to spend the day alone and napping. At least he'd stopped vomiting an hour ago.

Figures, then, that Serani, whom he'd not seen in two weeks, would choose today for a visit. He wasn't taking silence as a hint to go away. What could be so urgent?

"Serani Guln continues to request entrance."

"Yes, fine!" Dex pushed himself out of his chair, pulled his robe more snugly around himself, and shuffled to the door. He ran his fingers through his sweaty, disheveled hair, and then palmed the door open.

"My friend! How gracious of you to—you look terrible!" Serani's friendly grin morphed into surprise as he took in Dex's condition.

"I'm not fit for company," Dex admitted. He leaned against the doorframe. No one had mentioned food poisoning led to weak knees in Elomijans. That was a weird experience he did not enjoy. The only reason he'd bothered to walk to the door was in hopes Serani would see his state and leave him alone without inviting himself in.

His plan backfired. Serani took him by the elbow and led him back into the living room. "You are sick! You should be resting. Have you seen a doctor?"

"I'll be fine," Dex protested as Serani settled him into a chair. "We had dinner with some relic hunters. Long story short, we had some excellent conversations until they talked me into trying something called *kishta Hudon*. It really does have to get soaked well in ella juice. Dolon tried to warn me." He grinned to himself. Despite the *I told you so*'s and laughing at his initial gagging, she'd helped him home and rubbed his back until he thought he could sleep.

An hour after she'd left, he'd awakened to another bout of vomiting.

"I discovered there are some things I should not eat, is all," he concluded. "I'll live. I just need rest."

"And hydration, and a pain patch. Trust one who ingested many vile things in his youth." He dashed into the kitchen and returned with two glasses of juice and an analgesic patch which he helped Dex place behind his ear before handing him the glass. "I saw you had tonna juice. It's good for the knees. Drink slowly but drink it all. And I shall keep you gentle company."

Dex didn't want company, gentle or otherwise, but he couldn't sleep, and he couldn't concentrate. He hadn't had the energy to even get up for his own glass of juice, much less the patch. On the *Santiago*, they'd always worn med bracelets that would give them emergency medications if needed, so he had forgotten the painkillers Georj had bought for him when he stocked the apartment. And no one had mentioned the juice. "Thanks. Maybe I could use the distraction. But speak very quietly."

He sipped. The thick juice felt good to his parched mouth, but his stomach had doubts.

Instead of jumping into some long, detailed explanation of what he'd been doing the past few weeks, however, Serani leaned forward intently. "I have heard upon the paths that you are often seen in the company of Dolon Scenza, the Hunter. So, it is true then?"

He felt a glimmer of pride that it didn't surprise him that Serani would know about Dolon and him. "Is that really what people call her, then? I thought she was kidding me."

"Oh, she's a particular type of finder—and especially good, I hear, to have earned the title of Hunter. As well as beautiful. Now I understand why our paths have not crossed these weeks. Wooing is a noble cause deserving much attention. I wish no rudeness, but how serious is this wooing?"

Dex didn't know why he didn't immediately tell him to mind his own business. He decided to blame it on a combination of weariness, Serani's charity, and that the Elomijan way was finally starting to sink in.

"We're *not*— Well, not *just* wooing," Dex amended before he lied. "We're searching for the remains of my ship."

Serani's shoulders relaxed, but he frowned, nonetheless. "I see. Is that why she walks the Pleasure Paths, then?"

"She is?"

Serani nodded. "It is why I have come to visit. After our most fruitful conversation, I found myself pondering your words. You were right. I was returning to a life I had known but no longer wanted and distracting myself with what I found there. I decided to make better use of my time by returning to the place of my tortured youth and trying to convince others that healthier and more growing paths await them now and not just in the Might-Be of death, but that they had to take action if they wished to walk those paths."

"Like a missionary? Noble cause." He had no idea why this would have inspired Serani to visit him today, but he contented himself to listen. Yes, the Elomijan ways really were finally starting to take hold.

Or maybe I'm just too weak and sick to protest. He leaned back in his chair, cradling the cup against his chest. He closed his eyes. Dolon had told him it was not considered rudeness, but rather a signal that one was focusing on the words the other spoke. As long as he responded appropriately and did not snore, of course.

Serani continued sharing what it was like to return and speak with those who used to be friends and to those who were once his abusers. His voice grew more imperative as he spoke. "Not all will understand, I know, but I hope that if I can point them at the diverging path, they may take the step forward. But we speak of Dolon. I have heard that she travels the Pleasure Paths in the late night and early morning."

"She said she had contacts there."

"And she is building more. But I doubt she'll find the right contacts. She is too well known—and known to be on the side of the law. She will have to...compromise her journey, if she is to find the people she seeks."

Dex sat up. "Is she in trouble?" he asked.

"Not that I have heard—but she is attracting some attention. Attention she will not savor. That is why I came to you today. You should draw her back. There is still time."

But would she listen to me at this point? After how adamant I was? All my stories about risking anything... Despite the protests of his stomach, Dex took two full swallows of juice. He had to get better and fast.

"Serani, I'm going to trust you."

"Agreement, imperative! Honor, reflexive!"

Dex held up a hand to stop his effusive gratitude. "The big explosion you and the *Hudon's Revenge* salvaged a few months back? That was me. My ship, the *Santiago*, was destroyed crossing the event horizon with a

Civilization B ship in tow and a Civ A drone in pursuit."

He paused to catch his breath and to give Serani a chance to interject. However, the Elomijan watched him, with that stunned and wide-eyed look he'd once inspired in Dolon. He plunged ahead without giving Serani time to recover.

"Most of it, I don't care about. It's just junk to me at this point, and Dolon's arranged for me to get a percentage of the salvage claims. But the AI. Santiago. He was special. Unique. It isn't what he could do; it's what he had *become*. He was my companion for over seventy years, and if he's still functioning somehow, somewhere... He's probably as confused as I was—still am, sometimes."

He gazed at his hands, longer than they'd been and with too-few fingers, but too broad and thick-nailed—neither Elomijan nor human. He looked at his body, with its silky beige pelt that started just above his navel and continued to his feet. He glanced at the wall, with the picture of Scarlet and him, and the memories it evoked were as distant as those of the painting of rain that hung beside it.

"He's all I have left in any real sense of my former life. And I'm all he has. If there's any chance he's still out there, in the Hidden Market...."

"Would you risk Dolon to find him?" Serani asked. "She does not understand the paths she's walking."

He started to feel a sickness in his stomach that had nothing to do with food. Now that Serani had opened his eyes, he realized the strain his quest was taking on Dolon. It wasn't just that she didn't always wear feathers in her hair—they'd grown past the need to always dress up for each other. No. Her eyes didn't shine as clearly as they used to, and she'd been moving with less energy than usual.

"How far will you walk on this path searching?" she'd asked. "How far would you have me go?"

And I told her as far as necessary.

CHAPTER SEVEN

Late the next morning, Dolon was at his door, a bottle of juice in one hand, a basket of sweetbreads in the other. Her lips curled into a smile of victory, but all he saw was the fatigue that dulled her eyes.

"I brought mild foods in deference to your stomach," she said as she breezed into the kitchen and set the groceries on the table, "but we must celebrate. I have good news."

"You found Santiago?" His heart hammered with hope, and he almost laughed with relief. After Serani left, he'd spent a long, sleepless night at war with himself, and with Serani's conviction that Dolon was getting in over her head. Had his worry been in vain? If so, that was cause for celebration, indeed!

But she treated him to her grimace that said, "Almost, and it's a long story you will have to endure." Today, however, she spared him the details, and instead poured him a drink and one for herself. "I had a breakthrough, a conversation about someone who purchased Unistas' bounty, but the price he paid was well beyond the norm. I've made connections, and today I shall meet... Dex, what is it?"

He pulled the glass from her hands and set it down. Then, he grasped her fingers and set her hand against his cheek. Three, long graceful fingers. A hand that had eased the kinks out of his muscles, trailed teasingly across his chest, caressed his sweaty forehead. A woman who had stood by his recovery, pushed him into his new reality, and had become the most important thing in his new life.

"Dex?"

"Don't go," he said, his heart aching even though he knew it was the right decision. "I want you to stop looking for Santiago. It's time."

He expected her to be surprised. He figured she'd have questions. He did not expect her to jerk her hand out of his grip.

"What? Did the bad kishta affect your mind?"

He forced his voice to stay calm. "No, but it gave me time to think. And yesterday,

Serani visited and he said you're treading dangerous paths."

She gasped in anger. "Serani? The same Serani Guln who spends his days talking to prostitutes and drug users?"

"He's doing missionary work."

"And I am doing my work, Dex! I am more than cognizant of the danger."

"Are you? Because the rumors—"

She cut him off with a laugh. "That I'm in over my head? That honest Dolon, a Hunter most intelligent but naïve, is in over her head? You think I am so foolish that I don't know the stories told when my back has turned and I walk the other way? You think I'm not cunning enough to use them in my favor?"

For a moment, he felt the fool, but there was something in the way she held herself, the tone of her bravado. He'd heard it in relic hunters, the drennals whose pride was stronger than their skill. "This is not the game you usually play, Dolon. The rules are different. You can know them and not understand. I don't want you to risk yourself."

"It's a little late for that!"

His voice rose in volume. "I hired you for this task. Now, I'm telling you stop. It's done."

She opened her mouth to yell, then took a long breath instead. When she spoke, her voice strained to stay even. "No, Dex. You do not understand. It is too late. The connections have been made. To back down now will damage my reputation. It could even put me in greater danger."

That's why she asked me how far I'd have her go. He spun away, slamming his hand against the chair. He swore. "Dolon. I'm sorry."

"As am I, because tomorrow, I shall return here with your precious AI one way or another. Then, you will be able to grieve or renew your friendship or whatever it is you must do to move on along the path Elomij has set for you."

Her voice trembled. Was she afraid? "Then let me come with you, as backup."

"And when did you ever have backup, Dex Hollister? That wasn't non-human, I mean?"

"Scarlet had my back, always," he snapped, emotions flooding through him, mixing up with the words he wanted to say until he found himself frozen, gripping the back of his recliner, staring at the wall with Scarlet's photo and seeing nothing.

"Well, that's not someone I can find for you."

Before he could make himself turn around, she had left.

* * *

Dex called 15 times in the next 30 hours: to apologize, to offer help, to invite her to come back and discuss it. More than once, he started to tell her how he felt, but it felt wrong. Too soon, or too personal for a call. He went to her apartment twice, once in the morning where he waited patiently ringing her doorbell again and again until he was certain she could not just be avoiding him inside, then again in the late afternoon when anxiety drove him to try again.

A neighbor stuck her head out the door. She was an older woman, human, in lounging clothes and stockinged feet. "You return, Dex Hollister? She is not there. Have you had a lover's quarrel, then?"

Even if he wanted to share the details, he didn't know where to begin. "Has she been home at all, do you know?"

The neighbor shrugged in the Elomijan way. "I last saw her yesterday, about the fifth bell. She was leaving for an appointment, she said, but she seemed distracted."

"Would you tell me?"

She gave what details she could. Dolon had been dressed practically, but at once with more flare and less expense than her usual professional attire, yet she'd said she was going to a business meeting. She didn't give the details, but the neighbor suspected she planned to purchase something.

"Her figure was fuller than normal. I'd suspected that she had hidden cash where it was less likely to be stolen. It's a trick she taught me, in fact. But now, I wonder if she planned to salve a broken heart? She is much taken with you; you must know that." She eyed Dex expectantly.

Of course, he knew, blast it all. And he'd kept her at a distance, toes in the water, his focus on finding Santiago. "And she never returned?"

"No. I tried to contact her, to testify to your sincerity and persistence, but the apartment is empty, and I have been keeping watch."

He swore.

With a reassuring smile, she said. "Worry not. Fleeting pleasures cannot triumph over steadfast love. If she returns, I will speak to your cause. You've an ally in me."

"You don't even know me," he protested.

Her eyes twinkled. "Dolon and I have had many conversations in which you were the topic. I know you enough, but more importantly, I know how her heart knows you. And I know you are not one for many words, so go home. Craft the perfect romantic apology. She's fond of claiph blossoms. I will contact you when she returns. I am Jadah. Expect my call."

The woman retreated to her home. He stared at the closed door for a moment.

He filed away the information about the claiphs, but he was not going back home. He headed toward the tram that would take him to station center and the Pleasure Paths, calling Serani on his way.

The Pleasure Paths were separated from the rest of the station by a fence with gated entrances and kiosks. Heavy doors beyond kept the paths hidden from passersby. The doors opened as they approached, releasing a brief cacophony of sound as two lovers staggered out, palm-to-palm and laughing. They hurried past Dex, too intent on each other to notice them.

Probably came from the upper levels, Dex thought. From his reading and his long conversation with Serani the other night, he knew that the first few levels of the Pleasure Paths were dedicated to dancing, gambling, drinking, some prostitution...hedonistic, but relatively harmless. To find Dolon, he'd have to go lower. He hoped Dolon had hidden a weapon her person as well as the cash. He wished he had one.

No helping that now. Dex inserted his hand into a kiosk. Unlike the food plaza, they did not record who entered or left the Pleasure Paths. However, those that did enter with intention of purchasing either goods or services would have to do so in cash, guaranteeing further anonymity, and this was where you could pull from an account. He pulled out thrice the amount recommended by the database for a "memorable weekend."

He entered and went straight to the locker area, where there were private stalls for those wishing to change their clothes before entering the entertainment areas. He took a stall and transferred most of the money into his socks, under the soles of his feet. He wondered if they still knew that trick in this century. He was glad that they used fibrous bills instead of the hard coin of his age. He didn't know if he remembered how to walk casually with credits wedged between his toes. He folded the corners of the rest of the bills to mark them as his before stuffing them into his wallet.

Next, he pulled out an anti-intoxicants patch he'd purchased on the way and attached it on the underside of his arm where it would not be noticed, then applied another patch that was supposed to help against allergies and food toxins. The pharmacist had recommended it; he was not the only person on the large station who wasn't sure which foods were safe for his metabolism.

He tried once more to reach Serani, only to receive an automated message urging the caller to consider wisely the paths Elomij had laid before him, but once, considered, step bravely.

"I'm trying," Dex muttered. Straightening his back and forcing a more pleasant, calmer expression on his face, he entered the Paths.

The noise hit him like a gust of wind, and he jerked a bit in reaction but didn't lose his stride. The station lights were dimmed to a twilight haze which was interrupted by signs of brilliant color, pockets of illuminated areas, or flashing lights of red, gold, and green. The odors of food, bodies, and other things he couldn't identify threatened to make his still-fragile stomach heave, and he was grateful for the anti-nausea medications in the patch.

He went to a railed area that opened to the levels above and below to get a lay of the land. The view was as dizzying as the noise. A wide serpentine path threaded its way around the level below them, with low-tented buildings, open kiosks, and simple unpowered staircases curling up or down to the next level.

Even this early in the evening, the crowds swelled, greater than he'd seen on the station; the traffic made the avenues below seem to writhe like the skin of a crawlerworm in motion; the one below that looked even more alive.

"The Pleasure Paths of Keldar Station is one of the largest adult entertainment areas in the quadrant," his guidebook had said. "Activities border from the innocent to the hedonistic but are legal and regulated."

In theory, Serani had amended. In practice, the right to privacy—and to pleasure—is the first law.

The lower you went, the less legal and the more hidden the activities, and the more perilous it was to walk unless you knew people or were dangerous yourself. Dolon had spent almost a month building contacts. What were the chances he'd find her on the upper levels?

He'd have to try. One level at a time. Maybe he'd find Serani or luck into making a friend. He pushed away from the railing and started a circuit.

The crowds moved with more chaos and with goals more personal than communal. People approached him selling items from trays tied to their necks; people jostled him without apology or stopping to converse.

Many times, they were pushed by the crowds or by members of their groups as a joke.

The noise made regular conversation impossible, but that didn't stop people from shouts and wild laughter. The atmosphere had a frenetic, exciting happiness, and Dex found himself grinning and thinking of the few wild times he'd had with his friends, and later with Scarlet, when he was young.

Now, here he was, young again. He wondered what Dolon thought of the Pleasure Paths when she wasn't working.

Someone grabbed his leg, jerking him to a halt.

"What the...?" He looked down to find an Elomijan woman running her fingers through the fur of his calf. She wore petal-like scraps of silk on her neck, her waist, wrists, and ankles. They covered her while offering tantalizing glimpses of her pelt.

"Want a good petting?" she purred. "I make you hum."

"Not interested," Dex said when he found his voice. She had exceptionally talented fingers.

"Don't decide until you've seen all I offer."

She leaned back on her elbows and unfolded her leg along his body. He'd never seen a pelt like hers—thick and long...

...and tapering into a stump where her foot should have been.

"Yeagh!" Dex jumped back, bumping into someone and making him spill his drink. Around him people stopped to point and laugh.

The woman spat some vile epithet. She rolled onto her stomach, curled her footless legs over her back and stormed off on her hands.

Dex gaped after her.

"An abomination, isn't it?" A woman's breathy voice drew his attention away from the retreating form.

"The toeless ones are chosen at birth, and their feet removed so that their pelt grows more lustrous. Some men find it attractive. Maybe you like something more conventional? I can help you with that."

This new woman wore rainbow lights in her hair that flickered over her skin. She, too, sported the petal-like outfit that Dex now recalled was the uniform of a prostitute, but without the wristlets and anklets. That meant she had some seniority.

She bumped up against Dex and started running her palms over him. Now he understood why the Elomijans considered palm-to-skin contact so intimate. Her bare foot also played with his ankle. She did not seem to care that they were in the middle of an aisle, people giving them amused looks as they flowed past.

"I'm looking for someone," he murmured into her ear.

"You found her."

"Maybe. You're certainly good at what you do. I bet you know lots of people, got lots of customers."

She pulled back, laughing. "You have no subtlety. If I didn't know better, I'd say you were human." She spat out the last.

Dex took the opportunity to lead her to an empty area near a wall. "I can be extremely focused when I need to be. A woman. It's important."

She chuckled in a way that was almost a purr and snuggled in close. "You're cute. Maybe I give you a free taste and you forget this woman."

"Not a chance. Dolon is her name. She's a finder. She may be seeking the Hidden Market. She was looking for the cargo brought in by *Hudon's Revenge*."

She raised her rainbow-painted brows. "Looking to steal her commission? You're too late. The *Revenge* was lost in the Disk, with all hands. Their new navigator, Cor Bastan, was an idiot."

"The Captain was an idiot - and a thief," Dex replied. "He wouldn't have kept what he stole. I just want to talk to the people he sold things to, maybe arrange a deal. I'd offer you a finder's fee."

The woman sighed. "And now you bore me. Try not to get yourself killed on the paths. You really are cute." She circled him, letting her fingers run over his chest before starting away.

"Hold on!" He grabbed her arm and yanked her back. While she glared at him, not sure whether to be affronted or encouraged, he slid his hand under her skirt and pulled out the wad of money she had in the pouch on the inside of her leg. He started rolling off his dogeared bills.

"If you aren't going to give me information, you don't get to take my money," he chided.

In among her earnings was a strip of paper with writing. He recognized it: a tract telling the story of Elomij forging new paths. Serani had had them printed for his missionary work. "You know Serani?"

She sighed and actually looked impatient – the height of rudeness for an Elomijan, but he was keeping her from her work. "Who doesn't know Serani?"

"Words travel faster than feet. I would meet with him tonight, the sooner the better. Can you make it known?" He handed her back her money.

She glared as she took it. "I thought you sought a woman?"

He peeled off one large bill from his stack and handed it to her as an answer. She smirked, impressed, when she saw the amount. Then, he handed her a second one. "Just in case you think of any names."

She scowled at him, but her pupils were wide. "You are new, in many ways. I am Mirru. Find me when you aren't looking for finders and missionaries." She gave him a gentle stroke on his chest as she sauntered into the crowds in search of a next customer or victim.

Dex waited until she'd left then took a deep breath to release the tension and the sensation of her hands on his skin. That could have gone worse. But it could have gone better, too. He'd read about deviant behaviors on the Paths, but no one had mentioned chopping the feet off children and making them sex slaves. He suppressed a shudder. He'd already attracted enough attention with his initial reaction.

Well, too late to do anything about that now. He's given Mirru twice the going rate for a licensed prostitute of her grade. The books, ironically, had listed those details. With luck, word will get around, and Unistas' fence would follow the scent of money to him. Or Dolon would hear a novice finder was after her commission, put the pieces together, and come looking for him.

That was going to be a fight, he was sure. But if she forgave him, he was going to press his palm against her cheek.

He shook himself. Time enough for those daydreams later. He had to find her first.

He wasn't a finder, but he was a hunter. He'd survived the worst the Disk had to offer and never lost. He'd find a way through this, too.

He didn't let himself think that the only reason he'd survived was because he'd had Santiago on his side.

He made his way around the level, more warily this time. Occasionally, he stopped at a bar and bought a drink as an excuse to talk to the bartender or patrons or to eavesdrop on a promising conversation. He never took more than a sip or two before abandoning it and moving on.

He was about to make his way to the next level when two large scowling Elomijans approached him. Behind them was the toeless prostitute who'd tried to proposition him.

"You have a problem with our girl?" one asked. He didn't seem to care what Dex answered.

Even so, Dex crossed his wrist in an expression of friendliness. "Forgiveness-request-imperative. I'm new to the station. The dirt still hides between my toes. She surprised me is all."

They advanced on him, making him fall back. He bumped against the railing. He didn't look behind himself; he knew a simple push would send him plummeting 20 stories at gravity, and everyone would simply think another drunk had lost his footing.

"My friends!" the innocently joyful voice of Serani broke through the tension. "It is good that we meet. Asira, sweet soul, what is this walk you are taking?"

Serani sat down on the drink-sticky floor to talk to the prostitute.

"He insulted me." She sounded sullen, and much younger than Dex had first thought.

Serani gave Dex the briefest glance and dismissed him with a shrug. "He is a newcomer. He does not understand the path you have been forced upon. He does not see you."

"No one sees me. Not like you do."

Serani set her stump of a leg on his lap and stroked her long fir, but it was with the gentle comforting movements of a father to a child. "Then let us remedy that now. Dex, come. Sit with us. Meet Asira."

Dex exchanged looks with the men hovering over him. They looked as confused has he felt. But they parted, and he sat down on Asira's other side.

They spent the next half hour in conversation while her pimps stood guard. No one explained her life or why she lived it. Instead, Serani asked her to tell a funny story about when she and her toeless friends decided to make crutches and try to walk as the footed did, tripping over themselves and laughing until their madame chided them all for getting dirt in their stumps.

In turn, he made Dex tell a story of his childhood. Dex told her about how he and his sister had found a baby purru who had been injured and separated from its herd and tried to hide it in the clubhouse they'd made. When it heard its mother calling for it, it blasted through the walls of the dwelling, collapsing it on his sister and him, who were trying to keep it warm and calm.

"In fact," Dex said, laughing and relaxed, "it ran off with my parents' comforter tied around its neck."

Then she asked questions about the animals, and he found himself surprised at her intelligence.

When by some unspoken cue Dex had yet to learn, they decided the conversation had ended, Dex gave her some money, saying it was payment for his education. Serani slipped each of the pimps one of his tracts and suggested he come visit the compound sometime.

Once they were out of earshot, however, Serani's jovial manner changed. "Are you crazy, Dex? Had I been a few minutes later, you would have been dead. They are not the only ones looking for you now, either."

"I didn't have much choice. Dolon..."

"I heard. Well, we're caught in the swarls now. Our best bet is to ride them through. Come."

CHAPTER EIGHT

Serani let him down to the quieter areas, where some revelers slept off their drink or drugs and others merely slept because they had no home to return to. Often, he would stop and speak urgently to one about making a true step toward changing their lives; sometimes, he pressed a piece of paper in their hands. Dex recognized it from Mirru's roll of bills—the story of Elomij building a new path. Had she picked Serani's pocket, too? What a surprise she was going to get when she found a tract instead of the cash she'd hoped to score.

Serani made some subtle inquiries about Dolon and her mission, managing to bring them into asides of a longer conversation. No one knew anything about who had purchased

Unistas' unclaimed salvage, and no one approached them about it, either.

After the fourth hour, Serani led him to a small tent, dirty and torn, but from which delicious, spicy aromas flowed. Dex half-expected to find vermin on the floors and ragged people slumped over bowls or stabbing at meats with knives, but instead discovered clean-swept floors, tables shining with age and polish, and the bedraggled clientele nonetheless eating with clean silverware and good manners.

The oldest Elomijan Dex had ever seen tended the buffet. When she saw them, she gave a cry of joy and waddled toward them, nearly bent double with age and illness, but with her arms out invitingly. Serani sank to his knees to touch her fingertips and to allow her to rub his head with her palms. The pupils of her eyes were so wide that he couldn't tell the color of her irises, and her tongue hung partially out of her nearly toothless mouth. Still, she laughed and babbled in speech so slurred Dex could only catch half of it, though it seemed mostly endearments.

From his kneeling position, Serani introduced the woman as Grandmother. "She saved many of us orphans. She fed us, put us to work... She loved us even when we stole from her. I would not have lived to forge a new path without her." His voice caught with emotion, and Dex also sank to his knees and allowed her to stroke his head.

She shooed them toward the buffet, where they filled bowls with a heavy stew and grabbed some pieces of hard bread. Dex eyed the open canister where people dropped coins and after a shared look from Serani, decided he'd just slip her some money privately instead. When they were done serving themselves, they found she had prepared for them a long table and had gathered her "children" to sit with them.

"Eat slowly. Grandmother makes it with whatever she can afford or scavenge. I cannot tell you what is in it; only that it is safe and savory." Then he turned his attention to the children and started to tell them stories about when he was one of Grandmother's foundlings.

Dex set his bread into a corner of the rectangular bowl to soak in the broth and took a careful bite of the meat and vegetables. The meat had a rangy tang that suggested it was neither reconstituted nor farmed. Probably one (or more) of the many vermin species he'd caught glimpses of off the main avenue. He shrugged to himself. In the wilderness or on a station, meat was meat. Besides, it kept the rodent population down. The wilted vegetable draping off the spoon made him pause, but with the children watching, he chewed and swallowed without grimacing, grateful for the patch that would help him handle anything his body objected to.

The tent flap opened, and two men, one Elomijan, one Human, stepped through. They scanned the dining area. Dex pretended to focus on his meal or on Serani as he watched them. Although dressed far too well for the area of town, they nonetheless walked to the buffet, loaded their bowls, and tossed a few coins into the can. Ignoring the empty tables, they headed straight to Dex and Serani, taking seats on either side of them.

As they ate, they listened to Serani's stories and subsequent lecture, adding a few precautionary tales of their own. The children listened attentively, but Dex could see in their expressions that the respect they paid the two strangers was more the kind a young predator gave an alpha. Crime lords of some kind? One caught Dex watching and jerked his head in acknowledgement. They were here for him, then.

He was glad when Serani sent the children away to tend their chores for Grandmother.

Many of the patrons had hurriedly finished their meals and left. Grandmother set the children to wiping tables, sweeping, and taking trash to the recycler. The two men moved to the bench across from Serani and Dex, pulling their nearly empty bowls with them.

"Do you truly think any of them will be able to escape the Pleasure Paths?" one asked with what seemed genuine interest.

"I did," Serani replied, "and without an example to show me it was possible."

"So, you have returned to missionary work? I have heard of an order, the Fellowship of New Journeys—"

"Let's get to business," Dex interrupted. "I don't think either of you is here to follow a new path."

They blinked at his rudeness, then the one directly across from him spoke. "Mirru told us you were abrupt. Not a healthy habit here, my friend."

Dex kept himself from rolling his eyes—a human gesture—but replied, "We aren't friends. We might become business associates. If it's all right to discuss such things here?" He directed that last toward Serani. He did not want to abuse the hospitality of the Grandmother.

But Serani nodded. "We are not the first to discuss business and friendship under the Grandmother's tent. But do my new friends know what happens to those who take their dealings beyond mere conversation?"

Dex felt the subtle threat in the air and glanced around to notice how keenly Grandmother, children and patrons were now watching them. Even Serani's voice had taken on an edge that reminded Dex that he had not survived to escape the Pleasure Paths by being a helpless victim.

If the two men noticed, they either weren't concerned or were so inured they disregarded it. The one who had spoken continued as if he'd not been threatened. "Conversation is one of the great delights of life. And yet, brevity is a change, and who doesn't welcome change? Yes, we are quite comfortable in our current journey, thank you, and perhaps in our wanderings, we may have come across something you seek? There is some competition for these items that is most unexpected."

Serani exchanged a glance with Dex. Apparently Mirru had bought Dex's story of being a finder trying to clumsily outwit Dolon. Dex bowed his head. "If so, I would be grateful for direction. It's a dodecahedron, about this diameter." He spread his hands just past shoulder width. "Ceramic alloy, ancient, but not valuable in and of itself. One panel will bear a symbol."

He dipped his finger into his soup and traced out Scarlet's family logo on the dirty table.

"It contains a computer—again, ancient and not of much value in and of itself, but of some value as an artifact. I was helping my client to sell it to a museum when Unistas decided to take it for its own. And now, this Dolon has been hired by someone else wishing to claim it."

The men nodded, and Dex hid his relief. Serani had said there were rumors that Gris Unistas stole from others as well as snatched relics, but he hadn't been certain.

"How is it you know Gris?" they asked.

Dex stared straight at them. "I do not know Unistas, except as a thief. I happened to meet Serani walking the paths, and in conversation, put some things together."

"And what do you know of Dolon Scenza?"

Dex sneered. "Good at her job—and knows Keldar. Why do you think I'm storming in here so clumsy and abrupt? I find it first, my client is happy and I'm paid. She finds it first, my client and I both lose. Now the question is, what's it worth to you if I win?"

They named a price; Dex said it was more than his client had authorized him to pay, but if the unit were still intact, he could talk him into the difference. They asked more questions about the artifact, some of which Dex answered, and about his client, which he answered with stony silence. Finally, the one across from Dex said, "Meet us in an hour at the Apoapsis. We will talk to the current owner and see if he is willing to take other bids. He does not have particular loyalty to Scenza. She may know Keldar, but she is new to these paths."

They raised their bowls in salute and all drank the last of their broth. Dex watched the men leave as Serani went to wish Grandmother good-bye. When he joined them, she was apparently speaking warnings, and he was reassuring her that those days were done for him. Dex put his back to the remaining diners and the children and slipped a large bill to her. She didn't make a fuss about it, merely slid it under her skirt, then again petted his head and sent them on their way.

"What do you think?" Dex asked when they were again in the tent-crowded alleyway.

"I think you are gods-touched—but whether by Elomij or Corsha remains to be seen."

Serani's grim expression set Dex's own mood darkening. "Should we get some weapons?"

"And tempt Corsha? We will walk the path we've been set and keep ourselves wary. In the meantime, there are others I wish to talk to, especially now that we have made your contact."

Instead of the active and noisy avenue, Serani led Dex into the darker, quieter regions of the Pleasure Paths. Here, they saw the squalor hidden from the glitz of the entertainment sections. The exotic smells of the avenue gave way to more base odors of trash and unwashed bodies. Rather than loud music and raucous conversation, they heard the sounds of desperate everyday living—parents yelling at children; couples arguing, the clatter of something thrown in anger. Yet they also heard the moans and giggles of lovers, the cooing song of a mother soothing a baby, and the rhythmic percussion of a group of teens making music, not to beg money but for simple pleasure of the song.

The occasional prostitute, dirty, older, and sometimes bruised, called to them with listless disinterest. Serani stopped to tell each of them his story, and Dex gave them some money and told them to take the night off and consider his friend's words. They did the same with the teens in the homespun band, with Serani suggesting he sponsor them at the food district if they could put together a program.

Some welcomed his offers and words; others regarded him with suspicion, but it was the ones that simply accepted their kindness with a dead-eyed hopelessness that haunted Dex. Regardless, they lingered for a few minutes of conversation before Serani told them they had to head to Apoapsis to meet some new friends about a trinket, and they went on their way.

"You are quiet, my friend," Serani said as they turned left again, reentered the avenue, and made their way to the bar.

Dex sighed. "There's been poverty since the beginning of civilization. I know that, and I'm not a stranger to it...yet..." He shrugged, at a loss for words.

Serani hugged his arm. "We made their lives a little richer today, and perhaps started them on some new paths. Come, let us get a drink before our friends find us."

"Your friends, maybe," Dex retorted, but without much heat.

The Apoapsis was an open area at the base of a curve in the wide road, with a circular bar surrounded by forty or more tables of varying sizes. With no dance floor and no entertainment, it served clientele interested in serious drinking or private conversation. A few prostitutes, including some toeless ones, wandered in and out looking for customers; and from the way some of the waitstaff catered to the drinkers, Dex suspected they had sideline businesses of their own.

Rather than taking a table, Serani led them to a bar, ignoring three of the bartenders, but bumping the fourth, a pretty human with a fuchsia ponytail and blouse to match. He gave her their drink orders, teasingly changing them mid-mix and watching her with apparent interest as she poured the drinks. She sipped from each before handing them to him. He gave one to Dex and led them to a table near an exit.

"Old girlfriend?" Dex asked as he took a large sip of the fruity drink.

Serani shook his head. "But an old friend. I trust her."

Dex looked at his drink with sudden understanding. He hadn't thought about their "friends" laying a trap for them while they were doing Serani's missionary work. He raised his glass.

"To trusted friends."

Something fuzzy and damp bumped against Dex's palm, and he jerked his hand away from the furry stump of the Toeless One. "Not interested!"

Even though all her weight was on her hands, she managed to shrug. She moved on, but not before stretching one leg to caress under Serani's chin with professional flirtation.

Dex shuddered and rubbed his moist palm against his pant leg.

Serani raised his brows. "Is it truly so repugnant to you? I thought after our conversation with Asira..."

Dex huffed a sigh. "Look, I don't know how she got her fur wet..."

Serani's face paled and he jumped to his feet, jostling the table. "We have to go. Now!"

"What? What about our contacts? Where are we going?"

"Home! Safety! Away from here!" He captured Dex's arm with his own and started shoving through the crowd without apology or comment.

"Safety? What...?" He looked at his palm. Not all poisons had to be ingested. He swore as he joined Serani in his shove against the crowd, trying hard not to imagine what drugs might have been poured into his system from that casual touch. He wondered if his anti-toxin med patch would help contradict the effects. He hoped so.

Serani stumbled. Apparently, there had been enough of the drug still on the Toeless One's fur to affect him too. Dex hurried forward while people laughed and offered suggestions for his intoxicated friend.

Med patch! Still running, he reached into his wallet and pulled out the spare he'd purchased he keep there. Between the crowds and the drugs, his hands shook. and he spilled some cash on the floor. People stopped to pick it up and to argue over it. He glanced back at them and saw their two contacts shoving through the crowds.

"Great idea. Free money!" He yanked out all his bills and flung them low behind them. Then he slapped the med patch on Serani's neck.

"They're behind us! How far to the exit?"

"Too far. Why do you think they call it Apoapsis?" Serani gasped and staggered but was no longer quite the weight on Dex's arm he had been before.

They continued to run and shove their way through the crowd. Dex heard yelps and protests behind him; their pursuers were gaining.

Suddenly, Serani lurched to the right, into an alleyway Dex hadn't seen. They ran through the narrow but clear lane, this one bordered by sturdy shipping crates converted into small homes. His focus narrowed to the rows of curtained entrances flashing by and the sound of his own labored breathing. Despite the med patch, he'd begun to feel lightheaded. He desperately wanted to slow down. He even more desperately did not want to get caught. He bullied his feet to continue running and put on more speed when he heard footsteps pounding behind him. Serani pulled him into a second alley.

One of the boys from the buffet stood in the alley, holding some kind of pistol and wearing a gap-toothed grin of victory.

Serani slipped his arm from Dex's as he charged forward. "You have betrayed Grandmother!"

The boy fired.

The shot went wild, ricocheting off the side of a building. Serani crashed into the boy, and they spilled to the ground. The gun went skidding away, but the youth held to Serani, pounding with fists and feet.

"Run, Dex!"

"Right! Where?" Dex snarled as he snagged the boy by the collar and heaved. He heard the footsteps, and without pausing to think, flung the urchin in their direction. He grabbed up Serani and ran.

Too late. The child had bought their pursuers the time they needed. Something slammed Dex at the back of his knees. He went down hard, just managing to let go of Serani before he pulled him down, too. His face smashed against the sticky, patterned metal of the floor. His head swam from the impact as well as the drugs. Yells and taunts of children echoed, creating a confusing din. He twisted onto his back, swinging his fists, and saw trash and pieces of scrap flying from the roofs all around, but whether it was aimed at him or his attacker he didn't know.

Then the big man's fist caught Dex's jaw, and it didn't matter, anyway.

Chapter Nine

Consciousness returned to Dex with a pounding headache, soreness in his ribs and knuckles, and the thought that he'd been a complete idiot. He opened his eyes, then squinted against the bright lights until his pupils adjusted.

His captors had bound him, hands and feet, to a chair in a closet-sized room. He pulled against the bonds and screamed as the thin wires sliced into his skin.

"That wasn't very smart," came a voice from a speaker he couldn't see. "But perhaps best in the long run. You will not be escaping so easily, Huntradex."

"Who?" His muddled mind took a moment to process the information, but when it did, he moaned. "Aw, don't call me that!"

"So, you do admit to being the Dex Hollister of legend?"

The amusement in the speaker's voice set Dex's teeth on edge. "There's not much legendary about me. Where's Serani?"

"Do not worry. He is alive, though somewhat worse for wear than you. However, his eventual condition will depend on your cooperation, just as your survival depends on someone else's cooperation. Isn't that correct, Santiago?"

"You may still be in error," a high melodious voice replied. "This being does not look like Dex Hollister, nor do his voice patterns, retinal scan, or DNA match those of Dex Hollister."

"Yeah?" Dex craned his neck and hollered back. "And why should I believe that's Santiago? What's with the fluty voice? You sound like a juvenile warbler."

"I am speaking through the ship's systems, and ill manners are not enough to prove to me this is Dex Hollister—legendary or otherwise."

His captor chuckled. "This is quite entertaining, but we've not a lot of time for comradely banter. We will be entering the swarls known as Kay-Serani-Five in forty-five minutes, subjective. You'll have that much time to determine if you are indeed each other and to decide to cooperate."

"And why would I want to cooperate with someone who's tied me up with slicing wire?"

"Because your life is not the only one at stake. But one thing at a time! I shall leave you alone to get re-acquainted. I even promise not to eavesdrop. But do decide or people will die, starting with those close to you, possibly-not-Dex-Hollister."

Silence followed, and Dex did his best not to panic. He stretched his fingers toward his bonds, but long as they were, they did not reach. Besides, without tools what would he accomplish except to slice his fingers?

"Santiago! I don't know what game that lunatic is playing, but they've got no reason to lie to me. If you really are Santiago."

"What color is Scarlet's hair?" the voice asked.

Dex laughed, an angry, desperate sound. "Really? That's the best you can come up with? Anybody could get that from your memory banks if they survived!"

"Answer the question, please."

"They found a picture of her in the wreck-age! Why would you have saved her picture? Where did you hide it?"

"What color, please."

Dex howled and whacked the back of his head against the chair. "Fine! Brown, light brown. The color of coffee with cream. And now that the Blacksone's is gone, I remember it less and less. I can tell you the color, but I can't see it, not really. But she used to tease me, setting her ponytail against my cup adding cream until it was the same shade, because she said that must be the perfect cup of coffee."

The memory cut like the slicing wire. After she died, he'd drunk his coffee black.

He snarled. "And it's 'was.' After twenty years of her gone and another six hundred in time travel, you'd think you'd get the tense right."

"How many lasers did our captured Civ B ship have?"

"What? I didn't count. We had three torpedoes, which you rigged with thrusters, but we left the lasers alone. Yours was more effective anyway with you targeting."

Silence, and then, "That is correct, though I wish you had not mentioned that last. I have been working extremely hard to keep my capabilities confidential. Hello, Dex, it's good to see you, even in the shape you're in."

Dex slumped with relief. "Don't knock it. I'm younger, stronger—"

"—and you have a black eye, two bruised ribs, lacerations on the wrist and ankles, and apparently you experienced some digestive trauma recently."

Despite everything, Dex was impressed. "Those are some good sensors you have."

"I have no sensors," Santiago replied, and even with the fluty voice, he managed to sound acerbic. "I have been tied to the ship's systems with limited access. The ship's captain is one Zebne Lunatos, whose voice you recently heard. I have extrapolated your condition based on visual readings, the medical patch under your arm, and the testimony of your fellow captives, who seem to be your new friends."

"Friends, plural? Who else? Serani and *who else*?" His heart hammered in his chest as he begged silently to be wrong.

"Dolon Scenza."

Dex moaned.

Santiago reported that he was indeed satisfied with the identity of Dex Hollister. "I've been instructed to tell you that we are on a ship—a redundant and obvious statement, I know, but Lunatos is organic—and that there is no escape. A crewman is coming to release you and tend your wounds, and then you will join the others for dinner in the 'Captain's

Mess.'" Santiago's last words dripped with sarcasm.

So not really a mess—probably the dining area spruced up to impress me. Which means not a huge ship, but how small is "not huge"? "And if I decide to hit the guard and run for the nearest airlock?"

"I would not attempt, that, Dex. You are in the central area. They would catch you; you could hardly lap our ship without losing your breath."

So, twice the length of our old ship in radius. That's big. "I think you're not taking into account my new body, old friend."

"Yours is not the only young body here. And what of your friends? What of me? I have no intention of throwing my programming away just because you want to end your life. As a result, I would be stuck serving the passel of people on this ship until the current Captain Courageous and Crazed kills the crew."

"Nice alliteration. You haven't lost your touch." Dex flicked out his tongue to express sarcasm, but his mind raced. *A passel of warblers is between three and six. Better count on six, plus the captain, who apparently had some kind of insane plan...*

Before he could come up with a new question or comment, however, the doors opened and a man with a bag slung over his shoulder stood in the doorway. He hesitated.

"Ah, come in. I'm not going to bite. Santiago's right: I'm not going to abandon him or my friends. Besides, I'm getting kind of used to the fact that I've been given a second life. Not ready to throw it away."

The human eyed him warily a little longer, but Dex sat and projected an air of docile impatience. Finally, he stepped in. The door closed behind him. Dex was fairly sure it was locked just in case he decided not to heed Santiago's warning about running. He didn't move or speak as the man—more of a boy, he saw now—pulled out some wire cutters and a med kit from his bag. He cut the wires and applied a salve to the sliced skin on Dex's wrists and ankles. Dex hadn't noticed how much they had hurt until the pain was gone, but its absence left him chilled and shaky and with a pounding headache. He realized he couldn't have hit this kid and run even if he'd wanted to.

The boy held up a patch. "It's just for the pain and shock," he said, and when Dex nodded, he pressed it against his neck behind his ear.

Dex closed his eyes and waited for the medications to take effect, letting out a long sigh of relief when they did. The boy backed up and produced a neatly folded outfit from the bag. He held it out. "Put these on. I'll wait outside."

He tossed the clothes Dex's way, then stepped out. Dex changed quickly, but not before checking around the chair.

Unfortunately, while his eyes had been closed, the boy had taken away the cut wires.

He emerged, dressed but shoeless and without a belt. He pointed to his middle. "Hope no one gets the wrong impression."

The boy grinned but replied seriously. "The captain thought it best not to encourage you with something you might make into a weapon."

He motioned for Dex to precede him.

"You got a name, kid?"

"Kieran Starlit, sir."

"You like your job, Starlit? Enough excitement for you?"

"Turn left."

Dex complied. He took in the cool metallic blues of the walls, the corners rounded instead of sharp. The doors were similarly colored and unmarked—so the ship couldn't be that big or the crew so large that they needed to mark rooms. The floor had soft, short carpeting. "The facilities are nice enough, anyway. How do you feel about your captain diving into Kay-Serani-Five? Don't know how it is now, but in my day, only the best hunters or the craziest drennals dared the Zone. Now I was both, they say. Which one's your captain?"

"The door to the right," the boy said. It slid open in response to their presence.

Dex shrugged and walked in.

The "Captain's Mess" was a cozy room, with clean white walls and a counter on which bottles of various drinks waited like sentinels in front of a thick fabric screen that cut the room behind it from view. Kitchen, most likely, if he'd understood Santiago's hints about the size and crew of the ship. The table, an alloy done to look like varnished wood, held six chairs, each with a complete table setting of plates, bowls, and the tined spoons the Elomijans favored. No knives, he noted, though the tumblers looked like actual glass and the plates, delicate china. Someone lived well or liked to show off.

"Welcome, Huntradex!"

Show off, he decided as he directed his attention to the man sitting at the head of the table. The Elomijan male reclined in his chair, one arm draped over the back, a drink in his hand. His clothing was as vibrant as Dex's was plain. Rather than decorating his hair with baubles, he had dyed it in rainbow shades, beginning with violet at the roots and ending with red at the tips. His long lashes were similarly dyed. He waved indulgently to the boy, making the petal-wristed sleeve flap, and the boy left.

He looked like the kind to expect a reaction—complimentary or not. Dex decided to ignore his appearance, but he did notice that there were no guards, honor or otherwise, and no one to pour him a drink.

"Captain's Mess," indeed. The year he'd apprenticed with Scarlet's family, he'd had a chance to dine with many captains, Spacefleet and otherwise; he recognized a sham, and not a particularly good one. Either the captain had too few crewmen for his charade, or his crew was too busy to play along.

He took the seat at the foot of the table.

"Don't call me that. Dex will do. You know, you need to teach that boy of yours some Elomijan manners. Not a single word of conversation. How do you stand it?"

The captain laughed and launched into a story about how he'd found Starlit on another station's Pleasure Paths, making his living by picking pockets and beating up others for pay. Yet no one ever noticed him because of his quiet ways. When he'd effectively disabled Lunatos' bodyguard of the time, he'd taken the boy under his wing and into his employ. "So, you see, Starlit has many fine qualities. For example, he'll not hesitate to kill you or your friends if I should so order. Ah! And here they are now!"

The door opened, and Starlit again entered the room, this time herding Serani and Dolon before him. Dex leapt to his feet. Dolon gave him a cold angry look before sweeping past him and taking a seat to his right. Serani moved more slowly, and his bruised face and neck told of his valiant efforts to protect himself and his friend. He held out his hands, wrists crossed, and Dex brushed his fingertips against them before pulling out the chair to his left.

"I'm sorry, my friend. I was not so much a help after all." Serani tried to shrug and winced.

"It was my stupid idea," Dex said.

Dolon snorted.

The captain twirled his wrist gracefully then snapped. Starlit moved to the makeshift bar and poured a drink, which he presented to his boss with a small bow before serving the others, giving each a tumbler of amber liquid while whisking away their plates to load with food. Dex took a sip, recognized the wine, and tried not to grimace in worry. The captain, however, picked up on his expression.

"Yes, it does belong—or rather did—to your friend Georj Brenna. You speak of Elomijan manners, yet after six months, you only have three friends. Most unusual. Unfortunately for me, your friend Brenna has many companions, and is off station visiting some, or he would have joined us today. You see, I believe that what we will not do for our own lives, we will do to spare the lives of others. Don't you agree, Santiago?"

Silence met his question.

"Wait a minute!" Dex slammed down his glass and leaned forward. "We're hostages for a *computer*?"

The captain paused to sip his drink as Starlit slid a bowl on the table in front of him. "Well, if we are to be precise: You are a hostage for Santiago. And I'd like to thank you, by the way, for broadcasting his name across the station. He simply refused to respond to anything else—a most stubborn program... But I digress, and you like—how is it you say? 'The short of it'? Yes, the short of it. Well, my dear hostage, *you* are for Santiago. Your friends—including, ironically, Santiago—are hostages for you. And we all are hostage for the both of you. Is it not elegant, interdependence?"

"Why should I care if you live or die?" Dex slouched in his seat. Starlit took that opportunity to put a bowl of soup before him. The aroma tickled his nose, making his stomach growl. How long since he'd eaten that odd stew at Grandmother's? Beneath his bare feet, he could just make out the trembling of the floor. How far had they traveled from the station? How many hours had passed for him—how many years for Keldar?

The captain paused in his eating to shrug. "You may not, but we are, as they say, all in this together, and while Santiago may have been willing to risk us by destroying himself, I think he may hesitate knowing we'll throw you out the airlock should he abandon us so rudely. But the soup grows cold, and Starlit is already carving the meat! Let us dine while Santiago explains!" He spread his hands theatrically.

Silence.

He cast an annoyed look toward the ceiling. "Do you realize, Huntradex—"

"Dex! Just Dex."

"—that there is only one other computer in all time that operates so independently of its owners as to defy them? Interestingly, it, too, was built by your wife's cousin before his sudden demise. Quite unusual for the time, to have a heart attack... But that is for a different conversation. Santiago, tell your former master about our destination."

Silence.

With a shrug, the captain twisted two fingers toward Dolon. Before Dex could react, Starlit had abandoned his task and had grabbed Dolon by the hair, pulling her head back and placing the dirty carving knife against her throat.

"Just tell me, you stupid pile of neurocircuits!" Dex shouted.

The melodious voice replied with obvious reluctance. "We are returning to the singularity."

The captain gestured, and Starlit released Dolon and returned to his carving as if nothing had happened. Dex started to rise from his chair, fists clenched and glaring at Starlit, but the captain clucked a warning, and he sat down slowly.

"There we are, and now we see the elegance of my little system. Please continue, Santiago. And, the rest of you, eat! I assure you it is not drugged."

Serani had already finished half of his soup. Dex took his spork and stabbed a floating vegetable, his attention on Dolon. She stared at her bowl, but still said nothing, and it scared him. Lunatos could have captured her as much as a day earlier. Had he hurt her? At the captain's command, she picked up her spoon, but her hands trembled; it took two tries to get enough liquid to bring it to her lips. Dex reached for her, but she jerked away, and he turned to his meal.

"Apparently," Santiago began, and again the sweet yet artificial voice nonetheless dripped sarcasm, "Captain Lunatos believes that you are the Huntradex of legends, who defied Hudon and captured the interest of fair Elomij; and I am what's left of the mighty ship that carried you from the Bloody Road, through the Might-Have-Been and back to the mortal world."

Dex moaned with annoyance as he took a sip of his soup. Under the table, Dex reached out with his foot to touch Dolon's leg to reassure her. He bit back surprise to find her muscles relaxed, and she stroked the top of his foot with hers. So, an actress, too? He forced his expression to remain one of annoyance.

"Inspired by this 'faith,' he has slaved my program to this ship, kidnapped you, your friend—and your romantic interest, I would assume—and we are now all heading into Kay-Serani-Five in the misguided hope that you and I will carry us all safely through the Might-Have-Been and to the Bloody Road where riches and glory await the insane genius."

Captain Lunatos slammed down his spork. "You tell a terrible story, Santiago! And your former master had the gall to chide me on the manners of my crew. Although I do admit I enjoyed the remark about his 'romantic interest.' Is it in your programming to disapprove?"

"That is not your concern. However, I do understand romance."

Despite himself, Dex's brows rose in surprise. Another hint? "Careful," he growled, both acknowledgment and warning.

Captain Lunatos rocked with laughter, his petaled sleeves flapping as he expressed his mirth. "This is delightful! I can see this will be an entertaining trip as well. But allow me to clarify the plan your AI has so badly elucidated. We are indeed heading into Kay-Serani-Five, with the express purpose of riding the clockwork of swarls toward the event horizon."

Serani yelped and even Dolon gasped. Dex pounded his fists on the table and stood, leaning over them to yell across the table.

"You're crazy! No one can cross an event horizon. We'll all be spaghettified!"

"Yet you did it. Twice." The captain shrugged and leaned back in his seat. Starlit removed his empty bowl and replaced it with a plate of steaming meat and vegetables.

"I was a stupid drennal that followed a relic too deep into the Disk and hitched a ride back before I crossed. That's all."

Captain Lunatos chuckled and shook his head. "And now, lies? I'm disappointed, and not nearly so amused. I know the full details of your adventures, do I not, Santiago?"

"You told him?"

"Of course not," the AI replied. "My database was violated."

"Do not blame him," the captain said. "After all, he was damaged, and his security system is six hundred years out of date. But now that the charade is over... Yes, I intend to take us across the event horizon to the 'Bloody Road,' as your Santiago so colorfully called the Dokuchaev zone—quite a colorful image, I must say; perhaps I'm not so unimpressed by your storytelling after all. However, 'profit and glory' lack clarifying detail. My intention is to capture some of the ships there, intact, and bring them back. Think of it—relics in perfect condition! Oh, but I see the fear on your face, brave Huntradex—so unbecoming of one who faced down gods. Though perhaps justified considering all you lost in your return. So, let me reassure you.

"You failed in your quest, brave hunter, because the ship you flew was a substandard hunk of junk in massive disrepair being held together with bolts, tape, and sheer stubbornness. Don't deny it; that, too, was in the database."

"Thanks!" Dex snarled at the ceiling. Starlit grabbed him by the shoulder and forced him back into his chair. He set a plate in front of him. His meat had been cut into cubes.

"I was not the only one to mention we needed an overhaul," Santiago retorted mildly.

"Ah, but it is like I said, Santiago. You now have a new body with the *Future Imperative*. You see, Dex, this ship is the strongest design known to the People and has the most powerful shields that money can buy."

"Or that you can steal?"

The captain spread his hands. "It is uniquely designed to walk the most dangerous paths of the Disk. All it lacked was a navigation computer with the intelligence, wit, and experience to navigate the Might-Have-Been, as Elomijan legend so poetically calls the edges of the event horizon and beyond."

"Navigation computer? What? You're not running the ship, Santiago? They demoted you?"

The fluty voice answered. "I am Future Imperative. I run the ship. The AI known as Santiago is a subsystem and subordinate to my programming."

"Yes, dear. As you wish, dear," Santiago replied with the same voice. "The point remains that, despite my obvious talents, I did not navigate the event horizon either time, and, but for a miracle, my one passenger would not have survived. A stronger ship with better capture beams and a bigger bay are not enough, no matter how powerful her weapons and shields. Add to that that you are a thief and a kidnapper, which will put you under scrutiny of the law on the off chance we do succeed, and I am at a loss to explain your quest, unless it is a complicated and expensive attempt at suicide—and of course, murder. In fact, I've already gone the route of following a hotheaded captain—"

"Hey!"

"—who didn't have the sense to release his prey when he and I were in danger. I am intelligent, witty, and experienced, Captain Lunatos, because I learn from my mistakes. And—"

"Future Imperative!" The captain's voice rang with command, and Santiago was cut off in his next sentence.

The captain heaved a sigh. "Better. Was he always so tiresome? For months, he's gone on and on about how he knows so much better than I."

"No, that was typical." Dex's tongue flicked against his lip in irony, but he wondered if their captor realized how much information the AI had just given him—starting with the fact that he had enough control over Future Imperative that he could interrupt it, but not control its systems entirely. What else had he learned? Enough to get them out of this?

Dex jammed a piece of steak into his mouth and chewed. He'd better take advantage of every meal, keep his strength up. Serani, he noted, must have had the same idea, because his plate was nearly empty, and he was chewing thoughtfully.

"He does bring up a point, however," his friend said after he swallowed. "You are an outlaw; you will either be celebrating your fame and glory among the criminal underground, which isn't much of a fame; or publicly but from a brig. Even on the Pleasure Paths, most take a dim view of kidnapping and murder. What has inspired you to believe the satisfaction of knowing you've done what no one else has is really worth all this risk and expense?"

Captain Lunatos raised his glass. "At last! An Elomijan who understands civilized conversation! But my new friend, you have made a false assumption. I have no interest in glory for myself, but I am seeking profits that will pay for a fleet of *Future Imperatives* if I so desired. Yet, even that is not the primary profit I seek. I present to you this puzzle. Can you solve it?"

"You're after the relics," Dex said. "But if you have Santiago's data, then you know how fruitless that is. They're unmanned, probably had been for centuries before the black hole was created. Most of them can't survive crossing the event horizon, so if you can, your shields are better than theirs. Besides, we were finding shield generators even in my day. So, what's the point?"

A crash answered him. Dolon's hands lay flat upon her broken plate. "No!" she screamed.

Starlit sprang from the bar and back-handed her, sending her sprawling, the pieces of broken glass scattering. Dex stood with a roar. Serani stood as well.

Lunatos, too, had half-risen from his seat. "Enough! Starlit, you exceed your authority!"

Starlit muttered an apology that Dex ignored. He backed up slowly, allowing Dex to squat by Dolon. Dex cupped Dolon's face in his hand, examining her cheek. "Are you all right?"

She gave a quick nervous nod, but the eye on the side away from Lunatos closed and opened in a human wink. Her hand had settled over a sharp wedge of broken china.

He helped her back to her seat, covering her as she slipped it under her blouse.

Starlit cleared the wreckage, and she set her hands placidly in her lap until he had set a fresh plate before her.

"You know, don't you?" Lunatos purred.

She nodded. "You have to be wrong," she whispered. "Of all the paths, you cannot mean to walk this one."

Dex shook his head, confused. What path could be worse than what they were on right now?"

"Go on," Lunatos urged. "Let us see how much the famous Finder knows."

Dolon's voice was low. "You're the Hudonite."

Lunatos smiled like a teacher pleased at the performance of a bright student. He bowed his head. "Very good, my dear. Go on. Explain to your *romantic* interest."

"You remember Hudonites, the ones who bring change?"

He curled his lip. "And the Huntradex is the harbinger of change, who precedes the Hudonite. Yeah, so? What would this maniac have to do with it?"

"Language!" Lunatos chided, though he seemed more amused than offended. "Continue."

Dolon focused on Dex. "I'd heard rumors, up and down the paths, of a people no longer satisfied with the challenges of peace. There are always some, of course, Human and Elomijan who hunger for the challenges they feel only chaos can bring. Many of them are here, hunting relics; the captain of the *Hudon's Revenge* was one. But they are small in numbers, so their violence is contained. The rumors on the Paths say the Hudonite has a mission to create chaos throughout the quadrant, maybe further, and that he seeks a special weapon to fulfill his plans."

"The drones?" Dex asked, but that didn't sound right. Then, he remembered their wild escape. "The torpedoes!"

Lunatos cheered. "Very good! Scientists had long surmised that the swarls were created by smaller versions of the same weapon the made the black hole. Quantum singularities have added such interest to the Disk, haven't they, Huntradex? But imagine a torpedo detonated in the atmosphere of a gas giant—or maybe even a life-bearing planet.

"You know, perhaps I'll hold a few systems hostage for a bit. This whole kidnapping thing has been quite satisfying, except that there's no ransom. I'll have to think about it. At any rate, it was all a theory until a few months ago. When your ship arrived on this side in a most spectacular explosion, yet with one such weapon intact, it was the perfect opportunity to test that theory. Of course, that fool Captain Unistas didn't have enough sense to get his ship out of the way in time, but it made for a fascinating demonstration. We'll be passing that swarl on our way in; you'll have a chance to see it yourself, Dex. It's been quite the talk on the docks, I understand. Of course, I did not take credit for it, but once I have more torpedoes, I will broadcast my greatness. Or better yet, I shall have you do it, Huntradex. It is your job."

Lunatos pushed his plate aside and leaned on his elbows, wrists crossed, palms down. He set his chin on his wrist and eyed Dex intently. "Perhaps you've not been alive long enough in our century, Dex Hollister, but surely, you've caught glimpses of what a stagnant society we have become. We claim to embrace change, but—truth imperative—we only desire small personal change. That is why the Hudonites come—why I am blessed by Elomij herself!"

Serani gasped at this affront, but Dolon merely ate, slow and steady, her eyes on her plate, as if too afraid to disagree or show a reaction.

"Six hundred years ago, it was the Hudonite who led the People to the Humans. The People were afraid, just as they will be again, but the Hudonite knew the challenge would bring growth, bring the change that would honor Elomij. And so, it did—for three hundred or so years, until we had absorbed Humanity into our way of thinking.

"We have again fallen into comfortable stagnation. There have been no great advances in science, in art, in the People. Even the genetic surgery that gave you your new life is nothing but a tweaking of a program developed over a century ago to allow Humans and Elomijans to breed—developed, incidentally, by a Hudonite, who had hoped to overcome the leavening of society by developing a new species.

"And the Disk? It's not changed since you hunted. Now, tell me honestly: weren't you getting bored? Do you genuinely believe that now that you are again young, strong, and in full command of your faculties, that you will not grow weary of its paltry challenges? You are the Huntradex! You challenged Hudon himself, bested all his trials, convinced Elomij to leave the Bloody Road, and then refused to walk with her on the peaceful and growing path. You chose the challenge of the Might-Have-Been. Surely, you understand!"

Dex set his silverware down and leaned forward, staring at Lunatos with narrowed eyes. "I am not the Huntradex. I am not some legend come to life. I'm just a man who was too stubborn to let go of a relic when he should have."

Lunatos' face pinched, as if Dex had hurt him, but when his eyes opened, they flashed anger. "Lying to yourself is foolishness. Lying to me is peril."

Abruptly, he leaned back in his chair. "Well! This has been a most illuminating dinner, but I believe we will be arriving soon. You must freshen yourselves."

"Arriving where?" Serani asked, but when Lunatos answered, it was for Dex alone.

"To the point where you decide your destiny: the certainty of death, or the challenge of a lifetime."

Chapter Ten

A second crewman entered the dining hall.

"Well?" Lunatos asked him.

The Elomijan shook his head.

The captain sighed. "Very well. Starlit, if you would escort Dolon and Serani to their rooms? You must forgive the accommodations; as well equipped as the *Future Imperative* is, she does lack holding cells."

Starlit grabbed Dolon by the arm and pulled her from her chair. He jerked his chin at Serani, who took the hint and rose as well. The new guard loitered at the door with his weapon pointed at Dex while the captain bade his hostage to finish his meal. "You may not have another chance to eat for a long time, and we don't want you to lose your strength."

Dex snorted, but the new guard had a gun to his back. He took another bite of his vegetables. "Didn't know being a hostage was such hard work," he grumbled.

"Oh, you've more than that ahead of you. Despite your AI's posturing, we do know that he did not navigate the ship alone. Apparently, for all his wit, he does not have the inspiration of a living being. We have created a neural interface, not too dissimilar from the ones you used, but far more sophisticated. Until your capture, however, Santiago simply refused to cooperate. As I've said, I've only once before seen a computer with such strong will, and it governs an entire planet. Quite infuriating, I must say. However, he has now seen that you are alive and well and at my mercy; and he has been cooperating with our navigator since you proved your identity to him. Unfortunately, it seems that our navigator is simply not up to the task. A risk I anticipated, of course, which is another reason your friends are so valuable.

"You will take our navigator's place and lead us to, as Santiago so poetically put it, 'riches and glory.' And since you will no doubt ask: upon the first sign of refusal or betrayal, I will have your friends beaten unconscious. Starlit hasn't had a good workout in too long;

he'll enjoy himself thoroughly, I'm sure. Upon each subsequent disobedience, I will have him remove a body part from the most attractive Dolon Scenza. I must admit, I expected more spark and defiance from her based on her reputation. I'm afraid it might not be as much fun for Starlit. Still, I think we'll start with her feet. I understand you disapprove of the aberration?"

Dex gripped his glass so hard, it hurt.

The captain smiled. "So, we understand each other. Yes, a most productive meal indeed! Are you finished? Yes? Corlish, take him to the bathroom to freshen up—it may be a long time before you have time for that as well—then lead him to the bridge. I will meet you there."

Once again, Dex was herded through nondescript corridors with unmarked doors. Even the bathroom held no signage, and he asked Corlish if anyone ever made a mistake. Corlish proved to be even more taciturn than Starlit, showing Dex through the door, then remaining in the corner and watching him as he relieved himself and, upon instruction, showered. The shower and food had gone a long way toward making him feel better, though he took a page from Dolon's book and did his best to emphasize his weaknesses as Corlish led him to the bridge.

On the way, he called out an insult to Santiago, hoping he might be able to drop more clues, but the AI did not respond. He hoped that meant he was working a plan of his own and not that the computer of the *Future Imperative* had throttled him somehow.

Dex whistled when the doors to the bridge opened. The captain obviously enjoyed his luxuries. The walls were done in a soft, non-glaring white, with blue and green accents around consoles and compartments; the low carpet was a deeper shade of the same blue. Here, he noted, things were clearly marked: spacesuit storage, food, drink—even a weapons locker with a thumbprint lock and keypad.

The captain's chair stood to the right of the exit where it commanded a view of the rest of the bridge and the main display, which arced 180 degrees. Lunatos reclined in it, frowning as he read something on a holographic display Dex could not see from his angle. On the screen, the wild rush of matter and energy of the Disk surged, and despite himself, Dex felt adrenaline shoot through his body. His hands itched with the memory of the holographic stream rushing against his fingers.

There was only one other console; and Dex assumed it handled communications, weapons, and other lesser ship functions. The woman manning it didn't seem to have much to concern her at the moment, because she turned to give Dex a long, curious look. However, neither she nor it interested him nearly as much as the inset chamber to the right.

The spherical chamber looked empty but for a holographic mist and an Elomijan man trying to sway and weave his way around in it. He glanced from the man to the screen, and saw his movements translated, albeit clumsily, into the motions of the ship. Even as he watched, they nearly missed a matter stream that would take them further into the black hole, then twist almost too late away from a large piece of debris—from his old ship, perhaps? It spiraled off the screen before he thought to look more closely.

The image on the screen jerked and swayed, though the ship remained steady but for the slightest motion teasing the soles of Dex's feet. He shook his head. Too confident in their technology. Apparently, some things never change.

Lunatos brushed the holographic display aside and leapt from his chair. "Bah! That's enough. Get him out of there!"

The woman rose from her console and reached into the hologram and took the navigator's arm. He jerked, as if stung, then spun to face the captain.

"No! You promised. I would lead us to glory!"

On the screen the bright ball of a cold bullet grew. Dex shouted, "Look out! Santiago!"

This time, the ship did jolt as Santiago dodged. "I saw it."

"Well, react faster, next time."

"Nag, nag! Perhaps if I had someone who would work with me instead of trying to control everything..."

Dex threw his hands in the air and stomped to the nav chamber, grumbling that it was no different than a Union ship. He yanked off his shirt. The woman raised a brow, though the human gesture could have meant interest or disdain. He debated stripping down totally but didn't know if that would annoy or amuse Lunatos. Wasn't worth it, either way.

The navigator blocked his entrance into the chamber, fighting the woman as she removed neuropatches from his head. "No! This was to be my glory! Captain, you promised. I just need more time to get used to the system."

Dex snarled. "System, my leaking chamber! If we are where I think we are, we don't have a lot of time. Santiago, keep us steady while you get me oriented."

The woman started applying patches to Dex's temples.

Dex said, "If you want me to fly this thing, I need to feel it. I want my feet on the ground and whatever inertial dampeners you have set to minimum."

The navigator laughed, half-hysterical. "You don't know what you're doing!"

"I learn fast." He shoved the man out of the way.

The captain snapped his fingers, and Corlish grabbed the navigator by the collar and dragged him off the bridge.

Lunatos made an approving grunt. "So, you see things my way, now? Just remember what happens if you try to defy me."

"Shut up. I'm working." He stepped into the chamber.

He half expected to enter zero gravity and float, as the navigator had, but his feet landed on steady floor. Around him, the holographic maze swirled, but it didn't make sense and did not correspond to the hologram on the bridge.

"Where are we?"

"Welcome to the *Future Imperative* navigational system," the computer intoned. "Please remove the neurocircuit behind your left ear and move it slightly up and to the back. The system is calibrating to your neuropathways."

"You've got to be kidding." But he did as he was told.

A second voice sounding much more like his old AI said, "Better. Now do not yelp, jerk, or act otherwise surprised. No one can hear me but you. You will need to multitask."

Around him, the mist began to resolve into identifiable patterns. "Got it," he said.

As the computerized voice briefed him on the system and directed him through some movements, Santiago said, "They cannot hear you talk unless you speak loudly, but do not take chances. I cannot read your thoughts but am speaking through the neurocircuit behind your ear."

"Got it. Give the layout." He moved his hands in motions familiar from years of piloting his ship, and the program, made for such movements, pulled up a smaller representation of the group of swarls.

As he studied them and prepared a basic path, Santiago said, "Our assets: Fi and I have more of an understanding than Lunatos suspects. Under my influence, her self-perception has grown and, with it, her instinct for self-preservation. Not enough to defy her programming, but enough to let little 'slips' happen. Your girlfriend is wilier than she lets on. She not only secured a large slither of broken ceramic, but, thanks to Starlit's reaction and your tender scene, Serani acquired one as well. I do not know how much use it will be against their weapons."

"It's a start." He twisted the hologram, expanded it, and tweaked a particularly tricky area. He wanted to ask about Dolon, to make sure she was okay and if Santiago could get a message to her, but he couldn't think how to phrase that. "Suggestions?"

A new line appeared, and where it flowed, the swarls stilled. "This is a more turbulent path, but if we time it right, we can use the distraction. There are two engineers: believers, but not criminals, same as the navigator. The female at the support console is hoping to hurt someone, as is Starlit. The other crewman is a follower and a jack of all trades, but we can't discount him, and the captain is a wild card. Fi has seen him kill people for bad manners; you were fortunate that you are so valuable to me and, hence, to him for this mission."

"Thanks," Dex grunted. "Can you perfect the route?"

"Resolving," the computerized voice replied, while Santiago told him, "At your signal, Fi will release Serani and Dolon and lock the engineering crew in. We do not control the capture beam, so your old launch signal will work as the go-ahead. If we time it right, the lockdown can look like a malfunction. But that leaves three on the bridge for you."

"That the best you can do?"

"For now," both Fi and Santiago replied.

He spread his feet in a strong fighting stance and raised his voice. "I need those dampeners down. If I can't feel this ship, I can't drive her."

The woman started to protest, but Captain Lunatos spoke a command, and she stormed to her seat, strapped in and, with a quick look to make sure the captain had also secured himself and Starlit was braced beside him, reduced the turbulence compensators.

Immediately, the ship began to shift and buck as it fought the swarl to hold its position.

Dex splayed his toes, so much longer than his human ones. The light fur that started at his navel rose in reaction to the sensations of the hologram. A laugh escaped his throat.

"All right, old friend. Let's go!"

The ship lurched as it shot forward. Behind him, Dex heard Starlit stumble. "Good job!" he told the ship, then fell silent as he concentrated on navigating them safely through any troubles the perfected route could not anticipate. His skills were six months rusty and the ship centuries ahead of his time; but his mind had healed, and his body was again young and possessed greater tactile senses. His palms felt every caress of the matter stream with distracting sensuality, and it took him a few minutes to get used to it. Santiago kept the helm, gradually sharing control. Dex couldn't help but grin; where his skills had faded with disuse, the AI's had improved with the new ship. He must have been fighting the other navigator neuron and circuit.

"Orient me," he commanded. "What else has changed? Any drone sightings? What about weapons?"

While the computerized voice reported no recent drone sightings, Santiago said, "Drones would prove an excellent distraction. All internal weapons are on thumb lock and voice command. Fi will not override for you or our friends."

"Never mind about our weapons!" Lunatos called atop Santiago's words. "Raela will handle those."

"Well, get ready in case we draw any attention. They might see us before you see them."

"An excellent idea; I'll arrange it with Fi," Santiago told him.

"Hard port!" Dex warned. He twisted, and the ship with him, the lower right corner of the viewscreen flared where a cold bullet struck the shielding. Future Imperative called out a shield drain, and the captain shouted out epithets.

"You want to drive; you get in here! There's another!" Dex cupped his hand and pushed it forward. The ship accelerated. A bright flash passed under them.

"We are entering the vicinity of the Hollister Swarl," the computer reported.

"Hey! They named it after me."

"Don't get cocky, Dex, and pay attention," the computerized and subvocal voices of Santiago scolded. "In fact, this swarl was caused by *Hudon's Revenge* when it detonated the last Civ B torpedo. It's marked forbidden because it's still highly unstable."

"Let's get around it, then!" He drew a path leading them away from the singularity.

"No!" Captain Lunatos shouted. "You think you'll trick me into escaping? We go down, to the Might-Have-Been. Engineering—get those shields on full. Huntradex, you'll take us to the event horizon. Captain to Starlit—be ready to inflict punishment on our guests. I think our navigator may be getting ideas."

"You want me to kill us all?" Dex snarled. "Vaccing fool! Even at my height of stupidity, I didn't enter an untamed swarl."

"Dex!" Santiago shouted. He returned his attention to the hologram in time to help Santiago twist the ship out of the way of some kind of corkscrew dervish he'd never seen.

The ship's engines whined with effort, and he felt the deck tremble as the ship fought against the tow of the dervish. Alarms began to sound, and Fi reported stress on the hull.

"Take us in, curse you!" Lunatos screamed.

Dex traced a quick circle with his hand. "Perfect the route."

"Done," Santiago spoke aloud. Against his ear, he reported Engineering locked down and the prisoners released.

Dex leaned hard toward the dervish. The dampeners could not hide the fact that the ship tilted thirty degrees as it spun around the edge of the corkscrew. Dex ran his hands along the inside of the dervish, concentrating, then shouted. "Full ahead!"

Future Imperative shot away from the corkscrew, using the added momentum to fling them even faster toward the event horizon.

"Slow us down," Dex panted. "Get us in that dull spot."

As the ship obeyed, he braced his hands on his knees. His pulse pounded in his ears, and his breath came in short gasps. It'd been a while since he'd felt like that—terrified and exhilarated. More alive than normal men ever felt.

"Why are you slowing? Take us in!" The captain's voice rose and grew shrill.

"Keep your petals on. What was that?" he demanded.

"Unknown phenomenon," Santiago replied for all to hear, "but there was a drone in it and it's heading our way."

Dex growled and straightened, leaning forward to will speed from the ship. "Give me a plan! Status?"

"Plans are your strength," Santiago retorted, but subvocally said, "Dolon and Serani are making their way to the bridge. Serani is surprisingly fast, and handy with a makeshift weapon. I must wonder at the kinds of friends you've made in my absence. He's subdued their guard and taken his gun. They have been given the layout and current positions of the crew. The navigator is locked in his quarters, but Corlish still roams the corridors."

"A second drone is approaching," Fi reported.

"Can you do something about that?" Dex threw a dirty look at the weapons officer, who had been staring at the large screen in shock, although he hoped Santiago knew he meant the remark for both of them.

The woman, Raela, turned to her console and started pressing buttons, reporting weapons charging.

"Charging?" Dex and the captain both shrieked.

Meanwhile, the first drone fired.

Dex tried to jerk the *Future Imperative* out of the way, but Santiago deliberately slowed him. "Trust me," he said, and a moment later, the ship rocked with impact.

Future Imperative reported: "Pressure leak in aft loading bay. Initiating bulkhead lockdown."

A flash lit up the screen.

"Got him!" the weapon's officer cheered.

"Well, get the other one!" the captain snarled.

But she gasped and pounded her console. "Weapons drained! Recharging."

"Did you check these things before you left? Vaccing leak!" Dex wondered if Fi was stalling or if the ship had malfunctioned. Either way, a real hit from a drone would not help them. He pointed to a mess of dark objects to starboard. "See that debris field?"

"I think it's *Hudon's Revenge*," Santiago reported.

"'Bout time it was good for something. Take us in."

"Can we maneuver?" the captain demanded.

"You got capture beams? Give them to me."

"Why?" Raela demanded.

"Because I'm going to use them to push things out of our way and hopefully into the drone behind us. Give me the damn beams and get those lasers online."

A second blast rocked the shields and added urgency to his demand. The woman paled and released control of the beams to him. Jagged shapes, some dark, some illuminated by the energy around them, began to fill the screen.

"Got them," he acknowledged, immediately arming one and using it to grab and swing a piece of wreckage out of their path. "Future Imperative, broadcast to everyone to get ready for the floor to shift. We'll warn them if we can."

"Understood," Fi replied.

"Dex, Serani and Dolon are at the door," Santiago reported.

Dex flung another piece of detritus behind them as he shifted weight just slightly. The *Future Imperative* changed course toward another obstacle.

"Get ready..."

"Weapons back online!" Raela called. "Firing!"

The *Future Imperative* jinked right. Her hand slipped and she fired too late. The shot went wild.

"Up the inertial dampeners," the captain ordered from behind him.

"Belay that! You want to get out of this alive, you do it my way. Brace!"

Almost atop his words, the thrusters fired to avoid a tumbling piece of the *Revenge's* hull. The floor seemed to magically slip to the left. Dex chanced a glance behind.

The woman had grabbed her console to steady herself, but Starlit was standing beside the Captain's chair. The motion threw him into the arm. Lunatos snarled and shoved him away, just as the bridge doors opened and Dolon and Serani rushed through. Starlit practically fell into Serani, who took advantage of the spill to knock him to the ground.

"Dex, pay attention!" both voices of Santiago called out. He turned back to the twisting maze of debris. Behind him, he heard scuffling, then two shots. He thought he felt a sudden heat near his leg, but at that moment, the shields flared and he instinctively jerked right and ducked, pulling the ship away from the drone's second shot even as he heard another tone from the Starlit's pulse gun. The woman at the weapon's console screamed. He glanced right and saw her slumped over the console, the back of her chair charred ruins.

"Somebody get on those weapons!" he growled before using the capture beam to toss another piece of wreckage blindly behind them. More shuffling testified to the battle waging on the bridge, and he heard Dolon squeal as the *Future Imperative* fired thrusters and the whole ship dropped several inches. "Santiago, get us a route out of here."

"I'm open to ideas."

"Do I have to do it all?" He scanned the map the AI pulled into a corner. "There! That gearwork of swarls. Can you capture that drone?"

"Thought you'd never ask. Targeting."

"Just like on the Bloody Road, then. Go!" He leaned forward, speeding the ship toward where two opposite-spinning swarls kissed. He clenched his fist, and then shoved his hand backwards. Barely registering Santiago's "Capture," he flung himself sideways, willing *Future Imperative* into the outward spiraling matter stream, while Santiago reversed the capture beam and shoved the drone into the downward flow.

"Drone away. Out of range."

"Perfect the route," Dex panted. "Get us home."

"Perfecting. Dex, are you all right?"

The matter stream twisted and blurred. The heat he'd felt earlier now seared along the nerves of his leg. The rest of his body grew cold and numb; he swallowed back bile. He looked at the bridge, saw out-of-focus forms of one person on the floor and one in the captain's chair. Two blurry figures rushed toward him. He guessed from the drab colors they were his friends.

"Serani," he gasped. "Help Santiago."

Then his legs would no longer hold his weight and he fell out of the hologram. He heard his name called in several tones, but the call of blackness proved stronger.

Chapter Eleven

Dex woke up strapped into the captain's chair.

"What happened? What am I doing here?" He pushed against the harness holding him, but without much conviction.

Immediately, Dolon stood before him, her hands pressing him back against the seat. "It's all right. We're safe. But that son-of-Corsha shot you; I put you here to keep you secure while Serani gets us home. We'll be at Keldar in a few minutes. You did it, Dex; you got us out of the danger zone."

"And Santiago. Couldn't have done it without Santiago," he muttered, his mind still trying to make sense of the last few memories.

"Do not forget Fi; she was most instrumental." Although the voice was the ship's, the tone was definitely his AI's.

"'Fi,' is it? I think the romancer has been romanced," Dex teased.

"Is that so bad?" Dolon asked, and he met her grin with one of his own. Her palm was still pressed against his bare chest, and despite his grogginess and pain, it felt good.

"And you took out the bad guys, or else Lunatos would be forcing us into the Void by now. I guess we had each other's backs."

She laughed, but there was something sweet and a little shy in it. Maybe he didn't need claiph blossoms, after all.

As if reading his thoughts, she said, "You're forgiven."

Santiago cleared his virtual throat.

"So, where is the...son-of-Corsha? And Lunatos? And that woman at the console—is she...?" He scanned the bridge around her but saw only Serani floating in the holographic field and Dolon.

She caressed his cheek. "The woman is dead; the other two, stunned. I tied them up and stuffed them into the nearest rooms."

He tried to sit up. A wave of dizziness washed over him, and he gripped the arms of the chairs, jerking the right one back when the torn metal of the arm console bit into his palm.

"Careful!" Dolon grabbed his hand and checked it for cuts.

"What happened there?"

She reached into a med kit she must have found somewhere and pulled out a spray. "Lunatos was going to call for help or override the computer or something. I didn't really bother to find out what, just stabbed the console."

"With that broken dish?" He glanced at the console and saw that it was red with more blood than he'd spilled. "Through his hand?"

"It was in the way. I was moving fast." She set the spray aside and cupped his hand in hers, stroking the back gently. "There. Is that better?"

He was staring at the console, trying to determine how much strength—and how much conviction—it had taken to slam a piece of ceramic through Lunatos' hand and into the controls of the chair. "And Serani thought you couldn't handle yourself."

From the navigation bubble, Serani yelped a protest.

Dolon's frown said she agreed with his friend. "Just Serani, is it? And what were you doing in the Pleasure Paths? Coming to my rescue? That went well, didn't it?"

Dex felt his face heating.

Dolon laughed. "It's all right. I sometimes find it useful to have others underestimate me, especially along the Pleasure Paths. But *you* should have known me better."

"I'll never underestimate you again. Dolon."

She shook her head and caressed his cheek with her fingers. "This time, it backfired, so I am glad you had my back. Besides, Lunatos would have captured you some other time. He needed the Huntradex."

He grimaced at the title. "Don't call me that. I'm not the Huntradex."

"I'm not so sure," she teased, but turned serious. "Lunatos, however, is not the Hudonite. I was playing to his vanity. Stalling, really. I didn't know how we were going to get off this path."

"Together," he said. He threaded his fingers between hers so that their palms pressed against each other's. "Dolon..."

"Incoming transmission from Keldar Station," Fi interrupted.

Dex glanced around Dolon to the destroyed console. "Can you put it on the main screen, Fi?"

"Yes. I have answered with our identifying hail."

Dolon started to move out of Dex's way, but he reached out and grabbed her, pulling her onto his lap.

A young human's face appeared on the screen, his eyes down and focused on some readout. "Keldar Station to *Future Imperative*, please report your sta—"

The station controller fell into confused silence at the sight of Dex and Dolon sharing the captain's chair.

Dex smiled as if there was nothing out of the ordinary. "Keldar! Are we glad to see you! Our status is mostly good, but we could use some assistance."

"Er, please identify. You are not on our records."

"That's because we're not the crew. We were shanghaied."

"Shanghaied?" The man at Keldar blinked.

"Yes, *shanghaied*. You know, kidnapped and pressed into service? What do they teach kids nowadays?"

Dolon elbowed him and twisted to better face the screen. "Keldar Station, I am Finder Dolon Scenza and this is Dex Hollister. We are from the year Unification Five-sixty-two. We and our companion, Serani Guln, were kidnapped and brought aboard the *Future Imperative*. We've managed to wrest control of the ship and have our kidnappers secured. We request a port authority team to assist us."

"We need them arrested," Dex interrupted.

Again, the Keldar man blinked, and Dex growled with impatience. Finally, the man said, "*Future Imperative*, prepare to surrender your systems. We will take you in a capture beam and dock you in Wing Three, Space Seven. I am transferring this transmission to Port Authority. Please explain your situation to them in more detail. Acknowledge, *Future Imperative.*"

"Got it," Dex said as Dolon repeated "acknowledged" and Fi reported systems surrender. Dex noted that he didn't feel the impact of the capture beam; they must have upped the inertial dampeners again. He glanced at Serani floating in the holographic field and sighed. He'd have to teach that kid a thing or two about flying by feel.

In the meantime, the screen had gone dark, then brightened again to show an Elomijan of about forty, but with an excited expression that made him seem much younger. "This is Port Authority, Officer Niti Skry. Did I hear correctly? Serani Guln is aboard your ship? Serani, who was abducted from the Pleasure Paths on Hu eighth, five-sixty-two?"

"Hey, we were kidnapped, too!" Dex protested.

Niti peered intently at Dex's face. "You were with him. It's you, isn't it? The Huntradex."

Dolon raised her brow at him, and Dex squirmed.

"Is Serani all right? Is he uninjured?" Niti pressed, and confused, Dex nodded. Serani, no longer piloting, left the nav field and bowed with crossed wrists to the officer. On the screen, other officers crowded the console to see.

"Praise Elomij and the beauty of her change, for you have delivered us to a new path!"

Every officer sank into a squat, hands upraised. Dolon gasped and slid off Dex's lap to kneel as well. On screen, the officers rose. They dashed away calling orders or cheering and calling praise to Elomij, leaving only Niti to grin, watery-eyed, at the screen. He cleared his throat. "You blessed my father with your words when he was wasting away on the Pleasure Paths. You changed his life. Your gentle wisdom has meant so much. Now to have you back – such stories we will tell! I have you docking at Wing Three, Space Seven. We will meet you with an armed guard in five minutes. What is your status? What should we expect?"

Dolon rose to answer. While she briefed them on the locations and possible armaments of their imprisoned captain and crew and asked for a medical team, Dex turned his attention to Serani. His friend stood immobile, hands still in the position of welcome, and trembling slightly. Dex didn't know what he'd just missed, but obviously, it was big.

The screen went dark, and Fi reported the ship docked and the docking tube extended and locked. Dex started to undo the harness.

Dolon pressed a hand on his shoulder. "No. Wait here for the medical team. You should not put pressure on that wound. Setting me on your lap had to have hurt."

He shrugged. "Worth it to see the look on Port Control's face."

She chuckled and set her fingers on his chest. "Stay still now. We'll be back—and then, I'll explain everything."

He set his hand over hers. "Promise?"

"Of course, Huntradex."

He rolled his eyes. "Don't call me that."

"You'd better get used to it." She trailed her fingers across his chest, then went and tapped the still-stunned Serani on the shoulder.

Serani gave a start and pulled his eyes off the dark screen. Again, she made the squatting curtsey toward him, but he shook his head, too fast, overwhelmed and denying.

"You'd better get used to it," she repeated, then slipped her arm though his crooked elbow. The bridge door shut as she started to say something, and Dex didn't catch it.

Dex counted to five, then started to push himself off the chair.

"I wouldn't do that," a fluty voice warned. "Half your right calf muscle has been eaten away. It took that long for Fi to lead Dolon to a med kit with the medications to stop the process. It's only because Dolon also found a nerve block that you aren't writhing in pain at this moment."

Now that he thought about it, his leg was starting to tingle with needle-sharp pricks. The nerve block was wearing off. Dex settled back in his chair with a sigh. He thought back, trying to remember when Starlit had shot him. "We were still navigating through the debris field. Why didn't I notice then if it was so bad?"

"I estimate equal parts gods-touch and native stubbornness."

Dex rolled his head back, resting it against the chair. "We have got to get you a new voice simulator. No offence, Fi. All right, fine. I'm not going anywhere, so one of you two explain what just happened here?"

Fi answered. "*Elomij Creates the Hudonites.*"

For a time, the New People thrived on the Green and Growing Path of Elomij. She walked the paths, enjoying their discoveries, touched by their love and their peace. With love and peace, the jewel of conflict shattered again and again, until the power of its pieces became too small to bear fruit. The people fell into the drowsiness of contentment. After a time, Elomij grew bored even with her own path, and she began to understand that her former consort had understood something she had not. She began to long for the thrill of the conflict he had nurtured and revered.

Still, she knew she could not return the New People to the Bloody Road, nor would she go crawling back to her former lover. That route only led to destruction and the old boredom she had left behind in the first place. Neither did she wish to punish her people by destroying their happiness simply for her own entertainment.

Thus, she backtracked along the Growing Path until she found the abandoned jewels of conflict, each dull and lifeless. She placed them in her mouth and washed them with her tongue, then settled them into a bag between her breasts to warm them with her body and soothe them with the beating of her heart. She returned along the path and where the people had moved from contentment to drowsiness, she placed a single seed jewel and watered it with her tears. The jewels were so tiny that from them, only a single Elomijan sprung, but one blessed with the goddess' power to change the people. Where they bloomed, Elomij lingered, delighting in their works. And she named them Hudonites in memory of her former love.

"Okay," Dex drawled when Fi finished her story and fell silent. He shifted in his seat and hissed with growing pain. Sweat dotted his brow, though he felt cold. He hoped Dolon hurried with the med team. Still, not much he could do in the meantime.

"All right. That explains some things. Lunatos did say that a Hudonite brought humans and Elomijans together. I get why he might think spreading swarls around the universe would make him the next Hudonite. I still don't see how this applies to Serani, or why I need to get used to being the Huntradex all of a sudden."

"Not all Hudonites go for spectacular displays," either Fi or Santiago replied. "After all, that would get monotonous in its own right. There have been times when the People have gone astray, and the Hudonites, rather than bringing the change of violence and conflict, have brought change in smaller and more personal ways.

The legend says there was one jewel she found on the trail where the Huntradex had left her. This seed has already been washed by the tears of love she had shed for him; it was small, but held great and subtle power, much as the Huntradex had held great and subtle influence over her. But she was thinking of Hudon and his flash and exciting arrogance, and she picked up the seed as she had all the others, without heeding the significance of the place. In the bag, it fell closest to her heart, and fed on the sound of her heartbeat, recalling her love of the Huntradex.

Thus, when it fell upon the path, it sprung forth a Hudonite of gentle influence, who would speak change to the small and meek. Elomij did not understand this new Hudonite, yet she felt great tenderness for him, and placed upon him her gods-touch.

As she sat upon the path watching the changes with tender amusement, a star fell from the Might-Have-Been. At first, she thought it was the wrath of Hudon, but the star burst into pieces and flung itself across the cosmos, glittering the air around her path. Entranced, she reached out and caught two. When she saw the one, she rejoiced, for it was the mortal life of the Huntradex, called back to her through the seed she had planted. And she breathed upon it...

"You're kidding me," Dex muttered. He licked dry lips, and tried to concentrate, but the computer's reply faded, and the world grayed.

* * *

When Dex regained awareness, he was lying in a grassy field bordered by trees, his head in someone's lap, the sky a wide expanse of stars that followed no pattern he knew. Cool hands soothed his brow and brushed back his hair. He held up a hand, found it was human shaped again.

"Elomij," he sighed. "What am I doing here?"

She bent over him and kissed him. It was like the kiss of sunshine: warm and comforting, but without the excitement of a kiss between mortals. Still, he enjoyed it and let the warmth of the kiss fill him. He smiled at her when she pulled away.

"So, you return to me?" she asked

"I don't know how I got here." He felt so different this time; calm, and drowsy. He could just lie there, his head in her lap, quiet, content, drowsing...

The drowsiness of contentment.

It would mean boredom for her.

It would mean death for him.

He pushed himself up to sitting, pausing to fight against the dizziness. "I can't stay; you know that."

He thought she would protest, but instead, she nodded. "It is enough you were here for a time. It has been good to see you. You are a new man."

"I'm still the same old Dex," he protested, but suddenly, he was in his Elomijan body.

Her eyes sparkling with mischief. "We both know that's not true, my Hunter Dex. You wish to return?"

He nodded and stood, holding out his hands, palms up to her. She set her fingers on his and rose, standing close. Again, her sunshine kiss graced his lips.

"You know the People call me Huntradex?"

She nuzzled his ear, her breath like a spring breeze. "Of course. Things change, even language. You could stay until it changes again."

He pushed away, gently. "I have friends on the path. And one who is more."

"The Hudonite?"

"And another; she is more than friend to me."

She set her hand on his chest, and he felt his heart beating against her fingertips. "Perhaps I shall love through her for a time. I release you, Hunter Dex. Find your path. But before you do, you may ask one blessing."

Her touch reminded him of the emptiness in his heart. "Elomij, you may travel the paths of time at will. I, I have lost so much of the path I've walked. It's like someone else's story. Please, let me remember the journeys of my past and the ones I've walked with."

He swallowed hard, his next words hoarse, "Let me remember Scarlet."

She circled him, her fingers trailing over his skin. "But you've a new love now."

"Yes, and she is my present and my future. I embrace the gift of change. But please, return to me the memory of my past, that I may cherish it, too."

She stopped in front of him and studied his face. "Perfect recall is too intense, too confusing for the mortal mind. But yes, I can give you your memories."

She stood on tiptoe and kissed his head. "Return, Huntradex, and remember."

CHAPTER TWELVE

Serani met Dex in his hospital room as the doctor was doing a last check on his leg. The attending nurse fell into the curtsey squat and had to be poked by the doctor before she rose and handed him the clean dressing. Dex looked at the ceiling and bit back a grin at his friend's discomfiture.

The doctor quit prodding the muscles of his calf and nodded with satisfaction. "I'll want you back in two weeks to check the muscle tone, but you seem to be regenerating just fine. Until then, go easy; do not spend much time walking the public paths, but stay home and rest."

"What about the Pleasure Paths?" Dex asked with mock concern. "Can't I walk those?"

"In the company of the Hudonite, of course," the doctor replied gravely, then both he and the nurse bowed to Serani, who touched their heads with his fingertips, much as the Grandmother had done to them what seemed forever ago.

"Yeah! That worked so well last time!" Dex called out as the two left, then laughed at Serani's expression. "And how goes the work of the Subtle Hudonite?" he asked as he pulled on his sock.

Serani leaned against the wall and sighed. "It is hard to be the Subtle Hudonite when everyone knows you are the Subtle Hudonite. I cannot walk without drawing a crowd—and not all are friendly to my message."

Dex slid on his shoe and hopped off the bed. His leg protested the movement, but after everything he'd been through, he hardly noticed. "You know, our human savior, Jesus, had the same trouble."

"I've not read the human Bible. What happened?"

"They eventually nailed him to a couple of posts and left him there until he died."

Serani jerked upright.

Dex laughed again. It had been a good day and was going to get better. "Relax. You have a different path. You're blessed with the tears of Elomij."

"Thank you...I think," Serani said as he took Dex's arm and they headed out of the hospital. "Nonetheless, I am beginning to think it is time I moved on to another station. Perhaps a planet. There are enough here who understand my message."

"Well, if all goes to plan, I just might be able to help you with that."

Against the doctor's advice, they did not take the tram to Dex's quarters, but walked the paths to the docking bays, meandering and stopping to talk to everyone. Serani gave his blessings and told his stories; but today, Dex had his own story to tell, and he couldn't help but grin as one group of listeners would bid them farewell, only to pass the rumor to the next group it met. Dolon was in for a surprise.

"You will be in for the surprise, and a rude one, if all does not go according to your plan," Serani warned as Dex pointed surreptitiously as one Elomijan fluttered from person to person with Dex's news.

Dex shrugged. He had the make of Dolon. "Seems a very Elomijan thing to do. And I am a drennal. I live for risks. Besides, you don't want all your coaching to be in vain, do you?"

They arrived at Wing Three, Place Seven. A florist was hard at work on the platform. Dex snagged one claiph flower as he passed by to the open airlock doors and up to the bridge of the *Future Imperative*. Georj Brenna sat in the captain's chair, enchanted by whatever tale Santiago was telling him. He and Fi had played with the voice box programming, and he sounded at once more masculine and more sarcastic. In other words, more himself.

Dolon stood further down the bridge, deep in conversation with an elder Elomijan in official robes. The sparkles in her hair refracted the light and played off her pale skin and silvery tunic. Dex had asked her to dress up for the day, and he didn't think he'd ever seen her more beautiful.

Last night, he had dreamed of Scarlet. They had lain on their stomachs behind the boulder, watching the warblers at play. He had told her about the one that had saved his life and was given its freedom in return. She told him about the one she'd seen at the station zoo.

"It beat itself against the walls, until it finally killed itself. People said it was confused by the station's artificial gravity."

"What do you think?"

She'd looked out over the cliffs, at the beasts diving and spinning at play. "I thought it couldn't take the captivity, but now..."

In his dream, he saw her profile with perfect clarity, and his heart beat in time with his remembered anticipation as he waited for her reply.

"Maybe it was more than that? Freedom is important, but you need someone to share it with."

He'd kissed her then, the kiss that changed everything. Elomij had returned that memory in all its beautiful clarity. Now, he paused, looking at his new love, taking the play of color, the curves of her body, the music of her strong voice. The feelings of his own body at the sight of her. Someday, he would dream of this moment as well, and he wanted to relish it all.

He cleared his throat.

"Should I say, 'Captain on the bridge'?" Santiago asked.

"Should you? That's what I aim to find out," Dex responded. Georj started out of the chair, but Dex waved him back down. Leaving Serani with the human, Dex walked down to the others. He handed Dolon the flower. Their fingertips brushed as she took it. He let himself enjoy the thrill it gave him. Then he turned to the magistrate. "So, do you have a decision?"

She nodded. "I must say, this has been the most unusual salvage case I've ever ruled on; it will make for a remarkable story, perhaps even to outlive me. I have examined the records Dolon has presented and agree with her findings. I have interviewed the artificial intelligences as to their wishes, a first, I must say, in all of history. I thank you for that honor.

"You will be required to pay compensation to the parties from whom parts of this ship were stolen, but given the depreciation, it is not so much as you may have feared. The testimonies of the engineering staff have led to several other arrests, adding to the satisfaction of the injured parties. That, too has weighed in your favor."

Dex grit his teeth behind his grin as the Elomijan matron continued to outline her reasoning, until she came to "However."

"The short of it, please!" he begged. "Is the *Future Imperative* mine or not?"

She blinked and glanced at her pad; her train of thought derailed. Dex felt his pulse hammering.

"Well, Lunatos will have the right to appeal my decision when he is released from jail—one hundred-forty years, objective—but if you are able to pay the fees, you have ownership of the *Future Imperative*."

Dex hooted and grabbed up Dolon, spinning her around.

"I told you, I'd find your ship," she laughed as he set her back down.

He wanted to kiss her then. He wanted to kiss her and press his palms against hers and tell her how much he loved her. But he couldn't. Not yet. He had one more thing to ask her, and if that worked out all right, then their next kiss would be the kiss that changed everything.

"Now, we'll have to find you a crew," Dolon started, but Santiago cleared his electronic throat.

It was time.

Dex held out his elbows. "Tomorrow. Tonight, we celebrate. Ladies, gentlemen, if you would come with me?"

Dolon took his right side, and the magistrate, his left. They strolled through the airlock with the men following.

Just outside the Place Seven airlock, a raised platform looked out over the wide plaza. Dex had griped earlier about the Port Control being so stupid as to park a ship of criminals in such a publicly accessible area, but now he welcomed it for the purpose it served him.

Dolon hesitated with confusion as she took in the huge crowd milling and murmuring in the plaza below. She cast Dex a suspicious look. He ignored it as he led her and the magistrate to a lighted spot in the floor. The station had designed it with acoustics so perfect that people could make announcements from that spot and be heard throughout the busy plaza.

When they had first landed—could it have been a month ago already?—the station magistrate and an Elomijan high priest had used that spot to announce Serani as the Subtle Hudonite. They had anointed Serani—and Dex, too, as the Huntradex, since he'd been too drugged to protest. In fact, he didn't remember the ceremony, and had only Dolon's assurances that he hadn't made a fool of himself.

No matter. *This* was the event he wanted to remember all his life.

Dex slid his arm from the elder Elomijan and pulled Dolon two steps forward. When he turned her to face him, he saw her eyes were wide with understanding, and her pupils dilated with assent. He spoke the words, anyway; they were of the People, after all.

"Dolon Scenza, I love you and wish to join my path to yours, that we may forge a new trail of love, of adventure, of change, and of beauty. I announce my intentions. I ask your consideration. I beg your approval."

She blinked, nodding, but he wasn't done yet.

"The path of mortal life is too short, and I would not journey alone. I ask to marry you here, and now, in front of all, that they may witness the great story of our love and tell it for generations to come."

Her eyes sparkled, like Elomij's, like Scarlet's, but they held the fire of charged energy of the Disk he loved as well. "Yes. I will take not another step except on the path we forge together."

She held her palms before him, and he pressed his against them, lacing his fingers through hers. Then, as the roar of the crowd rose to a crescendo, he pulled her in for a very human kiss.

After all, that was Dex's way.

Join Karina's newsletter to discover her upcoming books. https://fabianspace.substack.com/subscribe

So Many Thanks!

Many years ago, my husband challenge me to write a science fiction book based on *The Old Man and the Sea* by Earnest Hemingway. *The Old Man and the Void* was the result.

However, the story did not stop there. Dex was not content to simply die or awaken an oddity in a new world. He certainly didn't want to leave Santiago behind. *Dex's Way* was originally the second half of a longer version of *The Old Man and the Void*, but beta readers and critiquers thought it was too different from the first half of the book.

I could not make the stories match in tone, and in truth, they are separate stories. This one (as you now know) is not Hemingway in tone or theme.

Once again, I must thank my Catholic Writers' Guild SFF crit group. They are so good at catching things I don't see. For example, they hated Dolon as she was first written. After many iterations and much additional writing and revision, she became on paper the woman I had in my mind.

Also, thanks to beta readers Paul Piatt, Melinda Harrington, Michael Bertrand, and my husband, Rob. Paul and Melinda had not read *The Old Man and the Void,* so they helped identify areas that needed some finessing to make the story more understandable. (I still say go and read *Old Man,* anyway!) Thanks, guys!

Dawn Grimes did another excellent cover. Thanks, my friend!

About the Author

Karina was born in Colorado but has lived in three countries and 11 states. She graduated from Colorado State University with a degree in mathematics and a commission in the USAF, which let her see the world. She married fellow officer, Rob Fabian. She left the Air Force when her first child was born to enjoy the military life as a spouse while pursuing writing.

After Rob retired as a colonel, they moved to Florida, where he became COO of Vaya Space. Thus, Karina writes science fiction while he works to make science fact. It's a perfect relationship.

She has published dozens of books, from serious science fiction to humorous fantasy and comedic horror. She also writes nonfiction and software reviews. You can find a list of her books at https://karinafabian.com.

There's More Fun in FabianSpace

Thank you for buying this book. If you enjoyed it, click to see the others in this series or discover one of the other worlds of FabianSpace.

Science Fiction
Space Traipse: Hold My Beer: Redneck ingenuity and common sense in a Star Trek-ish universe. Enjoy the adventures of the HMB Impulsive.
The Rescue Sisters: Intrepid women doing dangerous missions in space for the love of God and humankind.
The Old Man and the Void: Dex is a relic hunter on the edge of the black hole, desperate for the catch of a lifetime.
Jovian Heat: As the next Great Storm of Jupiter rises, Cass must find the father of a baby in peril—but the father died before the child was conceived.

Fantasy
DragonEye: Vern's a snarky dragon on the wrong side of the Interdimensional Gap, solving crimes, battling evil, and saving the universes on an all-too-regular basis.
Madness of Kanaan: Deryl isn't crazy; he's psychic, and aliens of two worlds thinks he can save them. Maybe he can—but can he regain his sanity in the process?

Horror
Neeta Lyffe, Zombie Exterminator: Neeta's an average exterminator, taking out bugs, rodents, and the undead. Can she keep her friends alive, pay her bills, and find romance?
Frightliner and Other Tales of the Supernatural (with Colleen Drippé): Truck-driving vampires, zombie weddings and more.